PUFFIN BOOKS

SUPER GRAN AT THE CIRCUS

The circus has come to town but things are fairly quiet in Chisleton; until the Scunner's life-long dream of becoming an ace pilot becomes a reality and he joins up with the RAF. Life in the forces is very different from the old films he's been watching on television – Flight Sergeant P. Brain will stand no nonsense and soon has his new recruit working really hard – peeling potatoes! Escape seems impossible until an old partner in crime needs his services to prevent Super Gran from turning Scousy's Circus (the worst in the world) into a success.

As the show goes on, Super Gran is flying high on the trapeze, showing off her Super-special powers – but does she know the rope holding the safety net has been cut? Can she save the circus, and save herself?

Forrest Wilson

SUPER GRAN
AT THE CIRCUS

Illustrated by David McKee

based on TV scripts by Jenny McDade

PUFFIN BOOKS

Puffin Books, Penguin Books Ltd, Harmondsworth, Middlesex, England
Viking Penguin Inc., 40 West 23rd Street, New York, New York 10010, U.S.A.
Penguin Books Australia Ltd, Ringwood, Victoria, Australia
Penguin Books Canada Limited, 2801 John Street, Markham, Ontario, Canada L3R 1B4
Penguin Books (N.Z.) Ltd, 182–190 Wairau Road, Auckland 10, New Zealand

First published 1987

Made and printed in Great Britain by
Richard Clay Ltd, Bungay, Suffolk
Typeset in 11/13pt Baskerville

Contents

1 Super Gran, the Scunner – and a Brain!

In Chisleton High Street a crowd of shoppers and passers-by gathered around as Super Gran apparently threw herself on to the ground head-first, then on to her back, then on to her side! But the crowd, at first alarmed that the old lady had finally gone bonkers, were soon cheering, clapping and shouting their encouragement.

'Oh, it's break-dancing she's doing, is it?' one of them said, relieved.

'Jings! Break-dancing?' Super Gran called out, as she spun round on her back, like a top, then stopped to get her breath back. 'It's more like "break-neck" dancing!'

'Come on, Gran, don't stop,' Willard urged her.

'It's all right for you,' she snorted, 'you're only playing "keepy-uppy".' Willard was ball-juggling with a football. 'That's easier than break-dancing, so it is. Next time we'll swop places and see how you get on with a sore back.'

'Well *she's* got the easiest job of the lot,' Willard replied.

He pointed at Edison whose task it was to carry a transistor radio to provide music for Super Gran's dancing, while also going round the spectators

with a can, collecting money for the Chisleton Old Age Pensioners' Club. And the dancing and ball-control exhibitions seemed to be very profitable, for before long the can became heavier and heavier.

'Wow! The pensioners are making a fortune, by the feel of this,' she said, after rattling it in the shoppers' faces.

But if Super Gran, Willard, Edison and the Chisleton old age pensioners were making money, the same couldn't be said of the Scunner who was broke, as usual. Not that he wasn't trying hard to earn some money, in his usual illegal way.

His latest ploy was to have his Muscles, in the guise of council workers, dig a deep hole in the pavement at the foot of the High Street. They placed a cardboard top over it, making it resemble a wishing well, in the hope that 'well-wishers' would throw lots of money into it so that their wishes might come true.

And, to add a bit of mystery and magic to it, one of the Muscles, Cedric, had been persuaded to climb down into it – and pretend to be a pixie!

After a few hours of this con-trick the Scunner, Tub and the other Muscle, Dustin, peered round the corner of a nearby building, watching to see how many mugs were parting with their cash.

'A wishing well is the next best thing to an oil well,' the Scunner declared, rubbing his hands together in anticipation of his expected fortune. 'Come on, let's go over and see how much we've made so far.'

After looking round to make sure that no one saw them, the Scunner, on tiptoe, led the way, with Tub and Dustin close behind him as he ran across to the well. They reached it and heard Cedric, from its depths, intoning: 'Pixie Pete will spin a spell if you drop cash in wishing well . . .!'

'Hey, Pixie Pete – it's us!' rasped the Scunner as he thumped the top of the well with his fist, to gain the Muscle's attention.

Then he popped his head over the edge of it, just as Cedric was popping his head upwards to see who was talking to him.

Now, usually, two heads are better than one, but not when they're in collision! There was a resounding crack, followed by: 'Ouch! Ooyah!' and 'Look out, ya buffoon!'

'Well? How much have we made?' the Scunner asked, as he massaged the pain out of his throbbing head.

'*Well?*' sniggered Tub, thinking the Scunner had made a joke. 'I get it! "Well!" Wishing well! Very good, Uncle!'

'I don't call this very good,' the Scunner snapped. 'Is this all you've made?'

Cedric had opened his clenched fist to reveal its contents: a few buttons, a couple of sweets from someone's pocket – with the fluff still attached! – and a Chisleton Athletic F C supporter's badge. It was hardly enough for the Scunner to retire on!

'You idiot!' He scowled, as if it was Cedric's fault.

He removed the man's hat and hit him on the head with it.

'I wish you wouldn't do that, boss,' he protested.

'"*Well*",' Tub smirked, 'that's someone who's "wishing"!'

As they walked dejectedly up the High Street the Scunner glanced again at the miserable earnings from their well stunt, which he held in his hand.

'Is this what I've come to?' he moaned. 'Is this all I'm worth? A handful of buttons? Doesn't the future hold anything better for me? Have I nothing to look forward to?' He was really depressed. 'I've achieved nothing in my life. Nothing!'

They passed Chisleton's TV shop but he was too busy feeling sorry for himself to notice he was walking on alone. The others had stopped to look at an old British war film which was showing on one of the sets in the window.

'There's surely more to life for me than a few measly buttons and some sticky sweets covered in fluff?' he muttered. 'Surely there's some way I could become someone important in the world? What do ya think, fellas . . .?'

He turned to ask the opinions of his faithful followers – and discovered they weren't faithfully following him! They were metres behind him, still staring avidly into the TV shop window.

'Huh?' he exclaimed. 'What's going on, eh?'

He retraced his steps to the shop to join them and saw, in the old film, two fighter-pilots complete with goggles and leather helmets, who were saying, in their English 'stiff-upper-lip' way, that they were going out to fight the enemy, and might not return.

'It's "scramble", Pinky. Time for off . . .' said one.

'Yes, old chap. And . . .' Pinky replied.

'Yes?'

'We . . . we may not . . . return . . .' There was a catch in Pinky's voice.

'Don't . . . don't say that, Pinky, old chap. Never say die . . .'

The Scunner stood transfixed at this Biggles situation, then pulled out a paper hanky to dab the tears from his eyes. Then he blew his nose, noisily.

Tub turned, looking puzzled. 'What is it, Uncle? What's wrong?'

'Wrong? Nothing's wrong, Tub. On the contrary everything's *right*. I know now what to do to become someone in the world.'

He pointed to the taller, more handsome pilot.

'That's Pinky Attenborough. My war hero. And I want to be like him. And *that's* how I'm going to make a name for myself. *That's* how I'm going to become someone in the world. I'm going to give up my tatty life of petty crime, and . . .'

'What're you trying to tell us, Uncle?' Tub interrupted. He was fed up with the Scunner's interminable speech-making.

'I'm going to be a fighter-pilot, like Pinky,' he said, at last, 'that's what.'

'What? But you get airsick going up on the

Big Dipper at the fun-fair!' Tub pointed out. 'Silence!' he yelled.

He wanted to enjoy the dreamy, fantasy thoughts he was having right then. Thoughts in which he was wearing goggles and a leather helmet and was sitting in an old-fashioned, First World War open-topped Sopwith Camel biplane, while a similar plane passed him containing another typical fighter-pilot who saluted him, and said:

'Carry on, Campbell, old boy! You're doing a grand job. Wizard prang! Pip, pip . . .'

He turned away from the TV shop and strode purposefully along the High Street, followed once more by his faithful followers. They passed Super Gran and company, who had now finished their stint at break-dancing and ball-juggling.

He saluted them and, for once in his life, wasn't the least bit nasty to them. He was pleasant. Or, at least, he was as pleasant as he knew how to be!

'Good day, dear little Super Gran. And you, my boy. And pretty little missy,' he smirked. 'My friends . . .'

His 'friends' turned to stare after them as they passed, and Super Gran shook her head in amazement.

'*Now* what's the wee bachle up to?'

The Scunner turned sharp left at the kerb, crossed the street and walked resolutely towards the RAF recruitment office, followed by his puzzled men. Then, after glancing in the window at the display posters, he entered the office.

Inside, behind a desk with a nameplate which read 'Flight Sergeant P. Brain' sat the Chisleton recruitment officer.

'Duck!' he yelled as the Scunner and his men entered.

'Huh?' they exclaimed, throwing themselves to the floor to avoid being hit by the deadly missile which had been aimed at them.

But the deadly missile turned out to be nothing more deadly than the paper plane which the flight sergeant had been in the act of throwing, with a cry of 'Wheeeeee!'

The floor around his desk, the Scunner noticed – after he and his men picked themselves off the floor! – was knee-deep in the litter of dozens of little paper planes he had been playing with. After all, he had to pass his time some way for there wasn't much doing, just then, in the RAF recruitment business in Chisleton. Not a lot of Chisletonians, he had found, wanted to enlist in the RAF just at the moment.

But then, remembering his dignified position, the flight sergeant hastily sorted through some papers and memos on his desk, adjusted his nameplate and tried to look busy, and as if he hadn't been caught playing with paper planes, like a little boy!

'And what can I do for you, sirs?' he asked, politely, smiling his sweetest smile at the newcomers.

'We've all come to join up,' the Scunner said.

'We've what?' Tub and the Muscles gasped, in unison, aghast.

That was the first they'd heard about this!

2 Riffraff – in the RAF!

'We've come to volunteer,' the Scunner said, ignoring the shocked looks on his men's faces. 'I want to have my very own Spitfire. Or Hurricane. Or Sopwith Camel, I'm not fussy. I want to be an air ace, just like Pinky Attenborough. He's my hero, you know.'

Brain grinned. These were his first customers in ages. He pushed enlistment forms and pens towards the Scunner and the two Muscles.

'Here you are, sirs. Just sign on the dotted line, if you don't mind. Thank you, thank you, thank you.' He rubbed his hands together and almost bowed over his desk to the Scunner, Cedric and Dustin. But he didn't seem to notice Tub. 'Welcome aboard.'

'I thought this was the RAF?' Dustin said, looking around. ' "Welcome aboard" sounds more like the navy.'

But the Scunner, though pleased, was taken aback.

'You mean, that's all there is to it? You'll take us – just like that? Aren't there any medical inspections? Don't you want to know how many GCEs or O-levels I *haven't* got, or anything?'

But Brain just smiled. 'No. No medicals, no GCEs, nothing. The Chisleton recruitment office hasn't had any recruits for yonks and we're desperate ... er ... that is ... um ... er ... we'll take anyone.'

The Scunner signed his name then pushed the others forward to sign theirs too, including Tub.

But Brain put his hand up in front of Tub's face and added:

'We'll take anyone . . . well, almost anyone. But you're overweight for the RAF.'

'Huh?' said Tub, shocked.

But he was even more shocked when the flight sergeant pushed him out into the street and locked the door.

'Hey! Lemme in! I want to join up, too. Make him let me in, Uncle . . .' he yelled, as he pressed his nose to the glass door, pathetically.

'Sorry, sonny!' Brain said, pulling the blind down so he wouldn't have to see Tub suffering outside.

'But why can't I join?' his voice wafted through the door.

'I told you, you're too fat,' Brain explained, then turned on his most oily smile at the Scunner and the Muscles behind him.

He gestured over his shoulder towards Tub, with his thumb, and explained: 'He won't fit into our planes, you see, till he loses some weight. There's not much room in our planes, nowadays.'

But Tub didn't give in as easily as that. He was determined. He beat on the door as if heartbroken at being separated from his friends.

'Lemme in! Lemme in! I wanna be an ace, too. An ace, an ace! Have a heart . . .!'

For a second it looked as if Flight Sergeant Brain

was going to relent. He smiled, pulled out a large piece of cardboard from under his desk and took it to the door. Then he opened it, thrust the card out and said: 'Ace? Here you are, chum, *you* have a heart!'

Tub looked at the large piece of card and saw it was a playing card – the ace of hearts! But before he could say anything Brain slammed the door firmly shut again, leaving him to walk mournfully away, thrusting the unwanted card into a waste bin.

He had never felt so dejected, or rejected, in his life. No one wanted him.

But why hadn't his uncle spoken up for him? He couldn't understand it.

The Scunner hadn't spoken up for Tub because he didn't want to say anything to jeopardize his own chances of enlisting in the RAF, and becoming an air ace like Pinky Attenborough.

He had signed the enlistment form and certainly been accepted, but it was just possible that the flight sergeant would sling him out again if he started to stick up for Tub and got the name of being a troublemaker.

He shrugged. Tub could take care of himself. And he, the Scunner, could always take him for a wee spin in his Spitfire, as soon as he got it.

And so, bringing his thoughts back from the unfortunate Tub, he joined the Muscles as the three of them, all highly excited, lined up in front of what looked like a serving hatch at the back of the office. Brain had briefly disappeared but the hatch suddenly opened to reveal him behind it, standing at a wooden counter on

'That's it, sir, you look very smart,' he fibbed.

Now, normally, after issuing a recruit's kit, Brain was supposed to stamp the inventory form to record that the complete kit had been handed out, as stipulated. But, in his excitement at actually having three recruits after such a long time, he banged the inked stamp down on the Scunner's hand, by mistake.

'Ouch!' the Scunner yelled as he moved away from the hatch, clutching his kit under his arm and sucking the pain out of his inky fingers.

'Next!' barked Brain, then added, more politely: 'Er . . . please!'

Cedric moved towards the hatch and saluted, poking himself in the eye as he did so! Brain quickly pushed his kit at him and then, by mistake, stamped him on the forehead with his inky stamp.

Then Dustin moved towards the hatch and, to save time, grabbed the stamp and stamped himself on the forehead with it – with such force that he almost knocked himself backwards off his feet. A gormless grin remained on his face throughout!

Presently, after the Scunner and his men were dressed in their uniforms, Brain dropped his bombshell: 'Right then, men, that's you in the air force – and you've signed up for twenty-five years . . .'

'T-twenty-five ye-years? Ye-yeeks,' exclaimed the Scunner. 'I didn't think I'd have to do that just to get flying a Spitfire. Pinky Attenborough never . . .'

'First of all,' Brain interrupted, 'you'll be posted to a basic training camp, to do what we in the services call

21

"square bashing". But before you go would you like to say goodbye to your loved ones? M'mm?'

'We don't have any loved ones,' Cedric said, sadly. 'We've only got each other.' He turned to the others. 'Ain't we?'

'Oh, come on,' Brain coaxed them, 'surely there's someone – some loved one – you'd really like to say goodbye to? Surely?'

He appealed to the Scunner.

'We-ell . . .' The Scunner gave it some thought, then said: 'There's always yon old bat Super Gran. Mind you,' he added, hastily, 'she's not exactly what you'd call a loved one, as such. But, well, all right, I'll go and say cheerio to the old bag o' bones.'

And he led his men out of the recruitment office to go in search of her.

'That's funny,' he said, looking up and down the High Street, 'she and her brats were here a wee while ago when we went to join up. Where's she got to?'

'There she is, boss,' Cedric said, pointing.

3 Black's Latest, Greatest Inventions

Super Gran, Willard and Edison were emerging from the Old Age Pensioners' Club, where they had been handing in their full collection tin.

'What's this?' she laughed, as the Scunner and his men approached, in their uniforms. 'What're you wearing those for?'

The ill-fitting uniforms – with too-long trousers, too-tight tunics and too-large berets – were not exactly high fashion!

'Are you going to a fancy-dress party?' Edison sniggered.

'No we're not!' the Scunner snorted, angrily.

'Don't tell me you've joined up?' Super Gran said.

Dustin grinned his gormless grin at her. 'Yeah, we all have.'

'So we're getting rid of you?' she asked. 'All of you?'

'Aye, except Tub, they wouldn't take him,' the Scunner said. 'But you don't have to be so pleased about it. We've come to say goodbye, and . . .'

'Oh rightio. Tatty-bye then,' said Super Gran, cheerily, then, turning to Willard and Edison she said: 'Come on, bairns.'

She swung on her heel to walk away, without a further word. But the Scunner was disappointed. He

had expected a fond farewell. And after all their encounters he thought he deserved a more tearful goodbye than that. He removed his beret and twisted it in his hands, emotionally.

'I'm going to be a fighter-pilot,' he said, trying to prolong the conversation while, at the same time, trying to impress her. 'With a Spitfire, just like Pinky Atten . . .'

But she interrupted him – by bursting out laughing!

'What – you? A fighter-pilot?' she roared. 'You're joking!'

Then Willard and Edison joined in the laughter and the Scunner was mortified.

'Well . . . ah . . . er . . . um . . . we'll be off, then,' he said, slowly, sadly. 'We're getting posted to our basic training camp. And then I'll be getting my Spitfire and my pilot's wings to sew on to my uniform.'

'Oh well, we won't keep you,' Super Gran called back over her shoulder.

'Yes,' Edison added, 'I suppose you'll have to *fly*! Ha, ha!'

The three of them laughed at this, but the Scunner's lip trembled as if he was about to burst into tears. He just wasn't getting the respect he thought he was due.

'Someday you'll read of my daring exploits in the local Chisleton paper,' he added, proudly.

'Jings! We're already reading about your exploits – in the *Gangsters' Gazette*!' she retorted.

But then, seeing his lip tremble even more and not

wanting a blubbering Scunner on her hands, she relented.

'Oh, all right then,' she grinned. 'Cheerio, you wee bachle – and good luck.' She walked back to him and inclined her face towards him, pursing her lips.

'What do you want?' he asked – dreading the answer!

'Aren't you going to give me a wee cheeper?' she said.

'What's a wee cheeper?' Edison asked Willard, who shrugged, puzzled.

'What?' thundered the Scunner. 'A wee cheeper? A kiss? Get lost! I'd need to be vaccinated first!'

Then he clicked his heels together, saluted and marched smartly back towards the recruitment office, followed by his two faithful followers.

'The air force must be desperate if they're taking the Scunner on as a pilot,' said Willard.

'Aye, but he always was a fly guy!' Super Gran chuckled.

'Talking of "fly guys",' Edison laughed, pointing to a poster of two men on a flying trapeze in a shop window they were passing, 'the circus is coming.'

'Let's go and see if it's here yet,' Willard suggested. 'It's up on the common.'

'Whose circus is it?' Super Gran asked.

'It's Scousy's,' Edison replied. 'I've never heard of it.'

'Are *you* coming, Gran?' Willard asked, eagerly.

'Not yet, Willie, I said we'd all go along to Inventor Black's workshop to see his latest, greatest invention.'

'Groans, must we?' moaned Willard who was less than thrilled by the idea.

'Aye, Willie. I said we'd look in for a wee demonstration of his latest inventiveness.'

'Huh!' he snorted. 'His inventive*ness* is usually an inventive *mess*! What silly gadget has he invented this time?'

'They're not silly gadgets.' Edison jumped to their defence. 'It's just that they don't always work first time, that's all.'

'Huh!' he snorted again, 'the first time they work is usually the last time they work, too!'

'I wonder what he's working on, this time?' Super Gran said, trying to keep the peace.

They found out as soon as they entered the workshop.

'I'm working on two different things at the moment,' Black informed them, absently, when they asked. 'Let's see now, I've got one of them, here in my pocket . . . The electronic bike, and . . .'

'Huh? You've got an electronic bike in your pocket?' Willard was amazed.

'No, you misunderstand. I was talking of two different things. That's the electronic bike over there.'

He pointed to a corner of the workshop where a streamlined racing cycle stood. The frame and wheels were almost entirely covered in plastic casing.

'What's electronic about it?' Edison asked.

'It's like a push-bike, with a motor,' Black explained. 'You don't have to pedal it. It works electronically – and it'll go like the proverbial clappers!'

'It'll go like the Super-clappers if I ride it, then!' Super Gran claimed, with an immodest smile.

'And what's the other invention?' Willard asked. 'Is *that* in your pocket?'

'Yes, it's a slow-motion machine,' he said as he fished a small, black object out of his overall pocket. 'It's as small as a torch or a pocket camera or a mini transistor radio . . .'

He switched it on – and a thin beam of light staggered out of it and a quiet, tiny, tinny voice announced: 'My batteries are nearly flat . . . My batteries are near . . . My batt . . .'

'Oh dear, this *is* the torch,' he muttered. 'The new one that tells you when it's running down.'

'Which it *is*!' Edison laughed.

He tried again. 'Ah, here it is.'

He pulled another gadget from another overall pocket and held it out in front of them. Then he pressed a button on it, there was a loud click and a tiny, tinny voice said: 'Smile please! Say cheese!'

'Oh-oh, that's my new super-duper camera,' he explained, after it flashed and they all blinked, blinded by it. 'Well, at least we've got a snap of us all together, eh?'

He pulled a third gadget from a third pocket and switched it on.

Super Gran, Willard and Edison waited patiently and expectantly for the demonstration to commence. But it was only when a loud, strident, tiny voice sang: 'Chis-le-ton Ra-di-o . . . sounds great . . .' that he

realized he'd pulled out his new mini transistor radio this time!

'Jings!' cried Super Gran, covering her ears from the sudden noise which assailed her Super-hearing. '"Chisleton Radio's sounds grate", is more like it!'

'That's it!' exclaimed Willard, who'd had enough of this demonstration. 'I'm going to see if the circus has arrived yet.' And he marched out of the workshop.

'I'll come with you,' said Edison, leaving Super Gran to suffer Black's demonstrations on her own.

'Humph! Cowardy custards!' she muttered as they left.

The Scunner and his men were lined up outside the recruitment office, in front of Brain. On the pavement beside them sat their kitbags containing their spare uniforms and civilian clothes.

'Right lads, are you all ready to be posted? Have you all said your last farewells?' he asked.

'Yes, sir,' they replied.

'Okay, but don't call me sir, I'm not an officer,' he explained. 'I'm just Flight Sergeant P. Brain.'

'Pea brain, did you say?' the Scunner grinned, but the flight sergeant ignored the comment.

He turned, looked over his shoulder towards the office, and yelled: 'Yoo-hoo, Pugh-hoo . . .'

At which their friendly neighbourhood postman, Postman Pugh, emerged and began to wrap large pieces of brown paper round the Scunner.

'Hey! What's going on?' he demanded, with difficulty

– as the paper by now came up to his mouth!

'This is you being "posted"!' Brain chuckled, as Pugh plastered the Scunner with sticky tape, and stuck stamps on him.

But, a few minutes later, after Brain, Pugh and the Muscles had enjoyed a laugh at the Scunner being 'posted', the wrapping was removed and Brain pointed to an open-backed lorry which was parked a few metres away, at the kerb.

'Right lads, your first-class transport awaits. Let's get you aboard.'

'Humph, first-class transport?' the Scunner muttered as the three of them clambered up and seated themselves on a bench along one side. 'I'll bet Pinky Attenborough never had to travel in an old heap like this!'

Brain fastened the lorry's tailboard, shutting them in.

'Right lads, you're off to RAF Paddleton, to do your basic training.'

'What? Paddleton?' the Scunner exclaimed, bitterly. 'But that's just a few miles along the road. I wanted to be posted somewhere more glamorous than Paddleton. Huh!'

'Oh, you'll enjoy your stay there,' Brain fibbed.

What he meant was: '*I* shall enjoy your stay there!' *He* was looking forward to it!

He then climbed into the cab beside the driver and told him to drive off. And as the lorry trundled down the High Street Postman Pugh saluted it on its way, while the Scunner was beginning to wonder if he had done the right thing in enlisting.

4 The World's Worst Circus!

Presently they arrived at Paddleton where they drove through the gateway, past the guardroom, and drew up on the parade ground, near the barrack huts.

But as Brain opened the tailboard, to let the recruits jump out, a sudden change came over him. He was no longer the polite person he had been at the recruitment office!

He threw his chest out, pulled himself up to his full height and rocked back and forward on his heels. And he lost his smiling face and pleasant manner as he shouted at them to join a dozen other newly-arrived recruits, from other towns, who were lined up and standing to attention.

'Right then, you cretinous morons,' he roared, in a completely different voice to the one he had used before, 'you're in the air force now – and you'll do exactly as I say. Understand? Get it? Right! Get into line there. Come on, move yourselves, move yourselves! What're you waiting for? Move, move, move . . .!'

'Huh?' said the Scunner, taken aback.

Behind him, he heard the gate at the guardroom being slammed shut, with a clang like the crack of doom. He looked back at it, panic-stricken, and felt as if he and his men were trapped. There was no escape for them.

What had he done? What had he let them in for?

And why was Brain shouting at them, like that? The Scunner hadn't expected to be treated like this.

Willard and Edison made their way across Chisleton common to where the circus was camped. A poster nailed to a tree advertised some of its attractions: Ethel and her elephants, Lionel and his lions, Tracy and her trampolines.

'There aren't many tents or caravans or things, are there?' Willard said as they reached the show ground.

'And the Big Top is more like a little top,' Edison pointed out. 'Is that the best they can do?'

It was small and shabby and was covered in tears and patches.

But while they were staring at it, in disappointment, a middle-aged man in a Tarzan outfit – a leopard skin and white tights – emerged from its canvas entrance.

'Oh . . . ah . . . er . . . um . . . customers . . .' he stuttered, obviously not used to having customers! 'Er . . . roll up . . . um . . . roll up . . . all the fun of the fair . . . Oh no, that's the wrong thing . . . Roll up, roll up, come along and see Scouse's Super Circus. There are seats in all parts of the Big Top. Hurry, hurry. Come and see our top-line acts. See the lions – or should that be sea-lions! See the elephants, the clowns, the acrobats, the . . .'

Willard and Edison exchanged doubtful glances as they looked all around and saw no one else in the silent circus.

'But where are they all?' Willard asked. 'Where are the animals and the performers – and everyone?'

'Er . . . well, I'm Sid Scouse, the owner,' the man introduced himself. 'And that's Wendy over there in the ticket Office.'

He pointed to a dirty, scruffy, paint-peeling box which stood outside the entrance to the Big Top.

'She hasn't been selling many tickets and she's down in the dumps,' he explained.

'It looks as if that's where they got the ticket office from,' sniggered Edison, quietly, to Willard. 'Down in the dumps – the rubbish dumps!'

'Yeah,' muttered Willard, *and* the Big Top, too!'

But Sid heard this and, looking pathetic, explained:

'You're right, but it's all I can afford. I'm down on my luck and I've had to sell all my good equipment – my Big Top, ticket office, tents and caravans – and rent this rotten old second-hand lot instead.'

'And the Big Top he rents – is full of rents!' Edison joked quietly to herself.

'But where are your performers?' Willard asked. 'The clowns and tumblers and tight-rope walkers and trapeze artists and strong men and . . .'

'That's them, coming now,' Sid replied, pointing to two men emerging from an old, rusting caravan at the edge of the site.

One of them had a black patch over his right eye and hobbled along with his left foot in bandages.

'Huh? Is that all?' Willard gasped. 'But who *are* they? And where's everyone else?'

35

'That's Walt and Pepe and . . . um . . . er . . . ah . . .' His voice tailed off as he admitted: 'Well . . . ah . . . that's all, actually. There *is* no one else. Not now.' He looked as if he were about to burst into tears. 'There's just them – and Wendy.'

Wendy was sitting inside the tatty ticket office, awaiting customers, and was polishing her nails to pass the time. She was middle-aged, like the others, and she looked up on hearing their voices.

'She also doubles as Juliana the juggler,' Sid explained. 'And Trudy the tumbler.'

'Hey, Sid,' her strident voice called out, 'are those kids buying tickets, or aren't they?'

'Er . . . um . . . er . . . well, I don't know, Wendy, my dear. Don't rush them.'

'But who *are* they?' Willard repeated, pointing to Walt and Pepe who were slowly approaching.

'And what happened to the one in the bandages?' asked Edison.

'Oh, that's Walt Wiggins, our Wild West trick shooter – from Wigan!' Sid explained. 'He's just been released from hospital. He bumped into the king, bashed his eye, couldn't see where he was firing – and shot himself in the foot!'

'The king?' said Edison, puzzled. 'What king?'

'Oh, that's one of the large poles that hold up the Big Top,' Sid explained. 'The king poles.'

'And the other one's Pepe?' Willard said, pointing.

'Yes. He's our Mexican performer – from Birmingham!'

'But that can't be the whole of your circus,' Willard said. 'There *must* be someone else!'

'No, not now,' he said, sadly. Then he addressed the men as they joined them. 'The four of us do everything, don't we, lads?'

'Yeah, boss,' Pepe replied. 'We do the lot. Good, we are.'

But good, they weren't!

'But what about the animals?' Willard asked.

'We don't have any, now,' Sid said. 'I can't afford them. It costs hundreds of pounds a week to keep them in feed alone.'

But Wendy, in the ticket office, was getting fed up with the idle chat and the lack of sales.

'Hey,' she yelled, 'are those kids buying tickets, or not?'

'You do want tickets, don't you?' His voice had a break in it, intended to gain their sympathy.

But Willard and Edison glanced again at the Big tatty Top, looked at each other, shrugged, and silently decided not to bother.

'Huh, imagine coming to this crummy old circus,' Willard muttered.

And Edison, hoping that Sid hadn't heard Willard's comment, said: 'But what about the other acts you've advertised? Like Ethel and the elephants, and Lionel and his lions?'

'They've been replaced by . . . er . . . ah . . . a French act. Henri and his horse,' Sid explained. 'And . . . um . . . very good it is, too.'

37

'Oh, a horse?' said Edison, frowning. 'But I thought you said you didn't have any animals?'

'Ah . . . well now . . . um . . . er . . .'

He coughed and cleared his throat but before he was forced to reply he was interrupted by Willard.

A sudden thought had struck him as he looked at the size of the Big Top, which seemed to be supported by hundreds of poles.

'But if there are just the four of you, how did you manage to put the Big Top up? It's huge.'

'Ah, well, you see,' Sid explained, 'I had a group of tentmen who did that for me. They erected the Big Top and fixed up the ring and the seats for the audience. And they rigged up the electric lights and the generator, and everything. But I can't afford to have them just standing around for a couple of weeks while we perform, so I paid them off.'

'But what happens when you move on?' Edison asked. 'Will they come back?'

'Yeah, well that's another problem,' he said. 'I'll hire them again – if I can afford to. And I'll only be able to afford them if I get audiences to come to all our performances. So you see the problems I've got?'

But Wendy, who had heard this conversation, yelled from the ticket office:

'What you need, Sid Scouse, to solve your problems is a miracle! And no one performs miracles, nowadays!'

Willard and Edison looked at each other. Super Gran couldn't quite perform miracles, but if anyone could help Sid, then she probably could.

'Give Willard some money for the phone,' Edison told a puzzled Sid, 'and he'll get you some help. And maybe even the miracle you're looking for!'

'Huh? Where from?' he asked, as he fished a handful of coins from his pocket.

'From Super Gran.'

'Who's Super Gran?'

Willard ran to the nearest phonebox, at the edge of the common, to persuade his Gran to come and help Sid and his not-so-super circus, leaving Edison to explain all about Super Gran and her Super-powers.

And this was just the chance that Super Gran was looking for – an excuse to get away from Inventor Black, who was boring her to death with all the details of his new inventions.

'Tell you what, Blackie, I'll try out one of them, if you like,' she said. 'I'll borrow your electronic bike to go over to the circus on the common. Okay?'

'Oh, rightio, Super Gran. The very thing. I'll show you how it works.'

Seconds later she was zooming her way to the show ground.

5   Super Gran, Circus Performer

Super Gran arrived at the circus and was introduced to its four members. Then Walt proceeded to demonstrate his Wild West act.

'And what does Pepe do?' Super Gran asked.

'He does a ball-balancing act,' Sid replied. 'Pepe! Show them.'

Pepe rolled a huge balancing ball out of the equipment tent. Then, while Wendy played a record of a drum roll followed by a clash of cymbals, Sid and Walt helped him to climb on to it.

'Watch this,' Sid said as Pepe was led towards a small see-saw nearby.

The idea was that Pepe would walk the ball up one side of it, over the top and down the other side.

They let him go and he was on his own. But not for long! For although his feet powered away like mad, he was unable to keep his balance and fell off, much to the amusement of Willard and Edison who howled with laughter.

While he picked himself up Super Gran jumped on the ball. Then she walked it, as if she had been doing it all her life!

'Gosh! Look at that!' exclaimed Sid, astonished.

'Och, it's easy-peasy!' she said, modestly.

Then it was Sid's turn. 'Come round here and I'll show you what *I* can do.'

He led them to the side of the Big Top where a tight-rope was rigged up for low-wire walking.

He climbed the ladder to the platform and, taking the long balancing pole which Wendy handed up to him, he started to walk the rope. But seconds later there was a howl as he lost his footing and slipped off it, the pole just missing the onlookers.

'H-help . . .!' he yelled, as he ended up, upside down, with his feet caught in the rope. 'Wendy! Walt! Pepe! Help . . .!'

'Jings! What a fankle!' cried Super Gran as she rushed to help the others disentangle Sid's feet and lower him to the ground.

Then, while Wendy applied bandages to his in-flamed ankles, Super Gran climbed to the platform and began to walk along the rope. She slid her feet forward as it bounced gently up and down with her weight.

'Look,' she cried, 'I've got the hang of it!'

'Yes, and Sid had the hang of it a minute ago,' Edison joked. 'When he was upside down on it!'

'Blimey!' exclaimed Sid. 'It doesn't take you long to learn things, does it?'

'Aye, that's right, laddie. It's being Super that does it.'

As she jumped nimbly to the ground Walt decided to demonstrate his Wild West knife-throwing act.

'Watch this,' he said as he produced his knives, to

toss them at half a dozen coloured balloons tied to a target.

But because of the eye patch he couldn't aim properly and, inevitably, the first knife he threw burst one of them, with a bang.

'Oh-oh,' said Willard.

'I hope you don't ask for volunteers from the audience to help you in that act,' Edison laughed. ''Cos you won't get many!'

'It's my turn, now,' said Wendy as she emerged from the equipment tent with a pair of high stilts. 'Watch this . . .'

She proceeded to totter around dangerously on them.

'I bet she falls off them within three minutes!' Willard whispered to Edison.

'I bet she falls off them within three *seconds*!' Edison retorted.

Edison won! Wendy fell off after taking only two steps!

But what was worse, she landed on the raised end of the see-saw, while Pepe was standing on the lowered end.

'Yeeks!' yelled Wendy, falling. And:

'Yeeks!' yelled Pepe, rising!

Walt Wiggins thought *he* was a Wild West shooting star, but right then Pepe was the shooting star — shooting into the air!

But Sid, ever the opportunist, put on his best circus showman's smile and said: 'Roll up, roll up . . . See Scouse's acrobats!'

43

And Super Gran, also the opportunist, grabbed her chance to have another go on circus equipment. While the others picked up the fallen Wendy and Pepe, she picked up the fallen stilts!

She'd had a go on stilts before, but these ones were much higher. And, as usual, she mastered them right away.

'Jings!' she murmured to herself as she looked at the others on the ground, far below her. 'Maybe I should become a circus performer. I'm better at it than that bunch, down there!'

She walked around on the stilts for a few minutes and then, as she jumped off them, Sid appealed to her and the children:

'Now that you've seen some of our acts, wouldn't you like to buy tickets for our first performance, tomorrow evening?'

'Look, Sid,' said Wendy as she went back to the ticket office, 'you're wasting your time trying to impress them. And they're not going to buy tickets for our performance after we've done it all for free!'

'But I *must* try to get customers,' he replied. 'I'll do anything to keep this circus going. The circus is in my blood.'

'If you're not careful,' Willard retorted, thinking of the performers' recent mishaps, 'your *blood*'ll be in the circus!'

Edison giggled as she had a thought. Show business people often said they were 'born in a trunk'. So, did circus people say they were born in an elephant's trunk?

And Super Gran also had a thought – that Sid's circus wasn't up to much. But she would never, of course, say so out loud.

Whereas Willard would, and did!

'Has your circus *ever* been any good, Sid?' he asked.

Sid was indignant. 'What? I should say! At one time it was really famous and ranked alongside the best in the country.'

A faraway look came into his eyes as his mind went back to his days of glory.

'Yes,' he continued, dreamily. 'In those days we had lots of big acts in the show. And Wendy . . .' He saw she was coming back towards them, from the ticket office, '. . . was young, and was really beautiful then.'

Then he spoiled this compliment by adding: 'But that was a long time ago, of course!'

'What? Cheek!' she snapped, huffily.

'What happened?' Edison asked.

'She got old!' he replied, misunderstanding the question.

'What?' Wendy stormed. 'You're no oil painting yourself, Sid Scouse. Humph!'

'No,' Edison explained, before Sid and Wendy came to blows. 'I meant – what happened to your circus? Why isn't it as good as it used to be?'

'It was all because of a London circus owner called Peck A. Daily – and his outfit the Peck A. Daily Circus!'

'Jings! It could be dangerous in the Peck A. Daily Circus,' Super Gran joked, but Sid took her comment seriously.

'Yeah, it is. They're a right rough lot. But they don't look it, 'cos they perform in the circus ring dressed as London businessmen – in city suits, bowler hats and umbrellas.'

'They must look gey strange, for circus performers,' Super Gran said.

'Yeah, but it's just their gimmick,' Sid went on. 'Except that they use their umbrellas to haul customers in to the Big Top! And their boss, Daily, as well as wearing all that city clobber, also wears his clown's "face" all the time, in the ring. I mean, even when he's performing other acts apart from clowning.'

'But he doesn't wear it when he's not in the ring, does he?' Edison asked.

'You know,' Sid said, thoughtfully, 'now that you mention it, I've never seen him without his clown's make-up!'

'But what did they do to your circus?' Willard asked. He was fed up with all these unnecessary details of clothes and make-up.

'Well,' Sid explained, 'everywhere my circus went the Peck A. Daily Circus went too. But they would get there first and pinch the best sites and steal our audiences. Or, if they arrived after us, they went round sticking *their* posters over *our* posters, or pasting "performance cancelled" notices over ours, to keep our audiences away. And they'd go about turning round signposts which we'd put up to point the way to our circus, and they'd make them point to theirs instead.'

'That's awful,' Edison sympathized.

47

'The wee cheat!' said Super Gran.

'Yeah. And eventually his circus was doing all the business – my business – and was enticing away not only my audiences but also my best performers, with offers of better conditions and bigger salaries. He could afford to pay them more than I could, from the money he made from my audiences.'

'That's terrible,' Edison said, when Sid finally ended his story, but Wendy only snorted, and said:

'Huh! *I* should have joined Daily as well, instead of hanging around here with *this* lot!'

She waved her hand round in a general way to include not only Sid, Pepe and the hobbling Walt, but also the tatty Big Top and the rusting cars and caravans which stood around. She shuddered.

'Aw, don't say that, Wendy, my little cherub,' Sid said, taking her hand. 'I've got faith in our circus. I just know it's going to be a top-ranking one again. I just know it.'

'Humph!' she snorted, taking her hand away, 'I'm not your little cherub. And besides, as I said before, it'll take a miracle to turn this heap back into any sort of circus again, let alone a top-line one.'

Edison took Super Gran aside, at this, and said: 'Well, Super Gran?'

'Aye, I'm not bad, lassie.'

'No,' she said, 'I don't mean that, I mean – well, Super Gran, do you think you could do anything for them? Could you work a miracle, somehow?'

'Jings, I don't know about miracles, exactly,' she

laughed, 'that's not quite in my line, you know.'

'But surely you can do something,' Edison persisted.

'I don't know what I can do, apart from performing for them You saw me having a go at some of their acts, and . . .'

'But what about all this?' Edison interrupted, waving her hand around to indicate the general air of tattiness and desolation of the whole circus area.

'I don't know what I can do about that,' Super Gran admitted. 'I think it's beyond even me!'

Edison turned back to Sid and company and promised: 'Well, you can rely on *us* to come to your first performance, anyway.'

'Yeah, if there *is* a performance,' muttered Wendy. 'That's at least three tickets we've sold. But if we don't sell any more there won't *be* a performance!'

6   The Scunner versus Brain!

The Scunner was addressing Flight Sergeant Brain.

'Listen moosh . . .' he began, but got no further.

'Who d'you think you're talking to?' Brain bawled. 'And who gave you permission to speak? *I* didn't.'

'Flight sergeants like to be called "chief",' one of the recruits whispered to the Scunner, so he tried again.

'Listen, chief . . .'

'And don't call me chief – we're not in the navy. I'm a flight sergeant, not a pretty officer . . . eh . . . I mean a petty officer.'

'But why are you shouting at us?' the Scunner asked, in a peeved voice. 'You didn't shout before, in the recruitment office. You were nice to us, then.'

Dustin turned to the recruit who stood beside him, nodded his agreement and said: 'Yeah, he was ever so nice, then. Yeah.'

'Ah,' explained Brain, nastily, 'but you were civilians then, in "Civvy Street". You weren't in the RAF. And I've *got* to be nice to civilians in the recruitment office – until they enlist. But once you've enlisted – that's different! I can be as nasty to you as I like, now!'

And he pulled off the Scunner's beret and hit him over the head with it, the way the Scunner was fond of doing to his Muscles.

'Ouch!' he said, and the Muscles sniggered.

But he wasn't so easily put off. He looked all round the camp.

'But where's my Spitfire?'

Brain's face turned scarlet, so he thought he'd better add:

'Or a Hurricane, I don't mind a Hurricane. Or even a Sopwith Camel, if that's all you've got. I don't mind, really . . .'

'Planes?' yelled Brain. 'You've got planes on your brains! That's the last thing you'll get your grubby little hands on. We wouldn't trust the RAF's extremely expensive aircraft on the likes of you, Campbell.'

The Scunner was shocked. 'What? But . . . but that's why I joined up. To get my own wee plane. A Spitfire or Hurricane or Sopwith Camel . . .'

'Listen, you soppy camel-face, get this into what you jokingly call a brain,' said Brain, 'Spitfires and Hurricanes are forty years out of date. And Sopwiths are about seventy years out of date. You're living in the past.'

'But . . .'

'And besides, you lot of little creeps are only the lowest, most contemptible, cretinous recruits in the whole of humanity. So there's no way you're ever gonna fly a plane. See? Now, that's the end of it. Left, right, left, right . . .'

And he marched them into their billet huts.

The Scunner and his men, having been allocated the same hut, were looking forward to having a rest to recover from the shock of finding out what the air force was really like. But inside their hut a dozen other recruits were already in residence, sitting around on chairs and beds.

'Hey, what are you doing in my hut? Come on, clear off,' he yelled.

Then, throwing his kitbag on to an empty bed, he muttered: 'Pinky Attenborough never had to share his hut with anyone! Huh!'

Suddenly the door flew open and Brain entered.

'Right, you lot – stand by your beds! Atten-shun!'

Everyone in the hut, including the Muscles, leapt to their feet and stood to attention, except the Scunner who did the opposite. He threw himself down on his bed, to be contrary. And besides, after such a tiring, frustrating day he *needed* a rest!

But Brain spotted him and charged across the hut. 'And what are we having here, Wing Commander Campbell?' he demanded.

'Three cups of coffee. How does that grab you?' the Scunner said as he leisurely raised himself on one elbow.

'And how does this grab *you*?' the purple-faced Brain retorted, catching hold of the Scunner and throwing him through the air to make him crash on the floor against a bedside locker.

Then Brain rocked back and forth on his heels and looked round the hut, at the others.

'Right, are there any more comedians in here?'

Presently the Scunner, the Muscles and the others,

after a short session of drilling, were only too glad to climb into bed and fall fast asleep. And that was only their first day – worse was to follow!

Outside the hut an owl hooted and a cat miaowed in the dark. But the owl and the pussy cat went unheard by the exhausted Scunner as he dreamed about the good times in his life, in Chisleton, where he didn't have the worries he had now. He'd only had Super Gran to contend with and she was tame compared to Flight Sergeant Brain!

He wondered if she was missing him but Super Gran, sitting up in bed in her nightie and curlers to wind her alarm clock, wasn't so much missing him as envying him!

'I'll bet he's having a real exciting time of it,' she sighed, wishing she could have the action-packed life he would now be having flying aeroplanes.

'He'll never want to come back to boring old Chisleton again.'

But she was wrong, of course, about the planes. *And* about his not wanting to return to Chisleton. He couldn't wait to return!

But he was going to have to wait, for Flight Sergeant Brain intended giving the recruits plenty of other things to think about! They would start next day – at the crack of dawn! – with the combined obstacle course and cross-country run.

The obstacles consisted of high walls over which they had to climb, broad streams across which they had to swing on ropes, narrow tree-top planks along which

54

they had to run and tight concrete pipes through which they had to squeeze. And the cross-country run was up and down the sand dunes of nearby Paddleton beach.

'Come on, Campbell, get a move on!' Brain yelled, encouragingly, when he got stuck in the narrowest of the pipes. 'Now you know why your tubby nephew couldn't enlist – he'd never have got through that one!'

And to show him that the Scunner was going to get through it successfully, Brain applied his large RAF boot to his rear-end!

'Ouch! Ooyah!' he yelled as he shot out the other end of the pipe.

'There!' Brain grinned, cruelly, 'I just knew you could do it!'

He laughed nastily and watched as they began their dunes run.

'Come on, Campbell, you've got another ten miles to go,' he yelled at the puffing, panting Scunner.

But Brain was giving his commands from the comfort of an RAF jeep which he drove round the course, while the recruits were being exhausted by their exertions.

'Wh-at?' the Scunner gasped, breathlessly. 'Ten mi-les . . . to go . . .? Puff, pant . . . Up and doon – these dunes . . .?'

'You're in terrible condition, aren't you?' Brain chuckled. '*You* don't get much exercise do you?'

The Scunner stumbled weakly over a little hillock as he looked across at Brain in his jeep. 'The only . . . puff, pant . . . exercise I get . . . gasp, gasp . . . is when I go

56

to the shop . . . puff, gasp . . . to collect my *Gang-sters' Gaz-ette* . . .'

Brain parked the vehicle at the foot of a sand dune and watched him disappearing over the top of it. Then he watched the stiff-muscled Muscles as they climbed the top of the previous one.

'Come on, you lazy layabouts,' he yelled, 'what's keeping you? You look like a couple of Girl Guides! Move yourselves!'

Presently the Scunner, sore all over, lay on his bed in agony. He had managed to sneak off for a rest when Brain wasn't looking. But he didn't lie there for long. Hearing the sound of approaching footsteps, he moaned:

'Buzz off, I'm exhausted. Bushed. Whacked. And I wouldn't get up, even if you were the marshal of the Royal Air Force!'

'What's that, what's that, you snivelling little oink? You despicable little toad? You detestable little horror?'

He looked up and saw it was Brain, of course. He sighed. Was he never going to get peace from him?

'Listen, laddie,' Brain said, 'the marshal of the Royal Air Force thinks he's the most senior man in the RAF – but he's not. *I* am! At least as far as *you* are concerned! Understand?'

'Yeah, yeah,' the Scunner mumbled, 'I understand.'

'I understand – what?' Brain prompted.

'I understand, chief.'

'Don't call me chief! I'm not a Red Indian! It's

flight sergeant,' Brain screamed. 'Now, get out of that pit!'

He grabbed the Scunner's bed and tipped it up until he slid out and landed on the floor, with a bang. Then he hauled him up by the scruff of the neck.

'On yer feet! Hup! Quick march. Left, right, left, right. At the double. Hup, two, three, four, hup, two, three, four . . .'

The Scunner meekly jogged from the hut on to the parade ground to join the others. But within minutes of joining them he had collapsed in a heap, utterly exhausted. And even when Brain bawled him out again he didn't hear one word of the harangue – he was fast asleep, and snoring!

Later, the recruits had combat training on nearby moorland with the Scunner and his men wearing camouflage kit and crawling on all fours across the rough ground.

'I'm knackered!' he moaned.

'And cold,' Cedric groaned.

'And hungry,' added Dustin, pulling off some of the leaves he wore on his helmet, as camouflage, to nibble them!

Suddenly a bullet whizzed over their heads and all three of them threw themselves to the ground.

'And that's something else I don't remember Pinky Attenborough ever having to do,' the Scunner protested, 'dodge the bullets of his *own* side!'

Suddenly some rapid machine-gun fire knocked Dustin's helmet off and sent it spinning into a muddy puddle.

'Right, that's the last straw! That's going too far!' the Scunner muttered. Then he stood up, to shout: '*We*'re not the enemy! We're on *your* side!'

But the only response he got was another burst of fire immediately in front of them, making Dustin jump into Cedric's arms with a cry of:

'Mum! They're killing us!'

Later, having completed their maneouvres and returned to the barracks, the Scunner stood in one of the shower cubicles, supposedly taking a shower! But he was too tired – or lazy! – to remove his beret and socks, which he still wore!

A trickle of water, hardly sufficient to dampen his big toe – but enough for him! – dripped from the shower. Then Brain entered the shower block and approached him.

'Ah, a good, strong shower will freshen you up, Campbell.'

He then deliberately – by accident! – switched the shower on to its full flow, and pretended to apologize.

'Oh, sorry,' he sniggered, as the Scunner looked up at the shower-head, swallowing about half its contents.

'Hey! Grooh! Glug!' he spluttered, between mouthfuls.

'What's the matter?' chuckled Brain. 'Don't you like being *Brain*-washed!'

'But I'm not due a wash!' he complained. 'I only bathe twice a year. On New Year's Day and my birthday.' This reminded him: 'Hey, I've just remembered – my birthday's in a few days' time. I forgot all about it.'

'I'd ask the cook to bake you a cake,' Brain sniggered as he walked away, 'except that the heat from all those candles might burn the barracks down!'

7 Scouse's First – and Last – Performance!

Sufficient tickets had eventually been sold for that evening's performance of Scouse's Circus to make it worth while having it. And Super Gran, Willard and Edison found themselves in the front row of the small audience. They knew what to expect from the show and they weren't looking forward to it.

'I'm not going to enjoy this,' Willard muttered.

'Me neither,' said Edison, making a face.

Suddenly there was a drum roll from the three old part-time musicians who called themselves the circus orchestra, and Sid strode into the ring in his ring-master's outfit to announce:

'Scouse's Circus is proud to present, live, from the Wild West – of Wigan! – Walt and his Whirling Whips . . .'

Walt came on dressed in his cowboy gear, his whips cracking the air above his head, to join his nervous partner Pepe who was already standing, quivering, in the ring with a stick sticking out of his mouth. Pepe just hoped that Walt could see properly despite his eye patch!

'Live from Wigan?' Edison whispered. 'I just hope *Pepe*'s still live by the end of the performance!' She giggled.

Walt cracked the whip and flicked it out, intending to flick the stick out of Pepe's mouth, but there was a yell as it wrapped itself lovingly around his partner's neck.

'Gug-ugg . . .!' Pepe gasped, half-choking.

'Is that what's known as a "whip round"?' Edison joked.

'Oh, sorry, Pepe,' Walt said, lifting his eye patch to get a better view of the damage he had done.

The audience laughed, then booed.

Next, Wendy entered the ring. She was dressed in a spangled circus costume, but it was one which didn't quite cover her mature figure the way it had covered it when she was younger and slimmer!

She attempted to do her juggling act but without success. She kept dropping the Indian clubs on her bare toes which were sticking out of her sandals. A juggler she was not!

'Ow! Ouch!' she yelped.

And her yelps of pain were accompanied by more boos from the unappreciative audience.

But at least this gave the others time to change from one costume to another. And then Sid's voice wafted out from behind a screen.

'And now, folks, the act you've all been waiting for. From Garlic-sur-Mer in France – Henri and his 'orse . . .'

At which Sid himself emerged from behind the screen dressed as a French onion seller, complete with onions hanging over the handlebars of an ancient, rusty bicycle.

Then from behind the screen there appeared a tatty old moth-eaten pantomime horse under whose skin Walt and Pepe could be partially seen, sticking out.

'And now,' he continued, referring to Wendy, 'my assistant, 'Arriet will ride the 'orse around the ring . . .'

Wendy tried to mount the horse, but failed.

'Maybe I should've stuck harder to my slimming diet,' she murmured to the two parts of the horse, as it – they – collapsed under her weight.

'*Now* look what you've done,' the horse's rear half accused its front half. 'You didn't support her properly.'

'*I* didn't support her? *You* didn't support her!'

And the two halves traded blows, under the skin.

At this Sid groaned, looked desperate and then quietly cried into his onions, while the audience booed and threw their ices, cartons of popcorn and programmes at the performers.

Super Gran shook her head sadly and turned to the children.

'Jings! Helping Sid and his circus will be a big job. It looks as if I'd have to do *all* their acts for them.'

The angry audience now scrambled out of their seats and ran to the ticket office but Wendy ran ahead of them, to defend it.

'Give us our money back!' they demanded.

'Your show's rubbish, missis!'

'You've got a cheek to call it a circus!'

She looked towards Sid, struggling his way through

64

the crowd, to get his permission to refund the entrance money.

Then, once it had all been returned and the audience had left, he mournfully announced: 'Well folks, it looks as if the curtain has finally fallen on Scouse's Circus.'

'But what about Super Gran?' asked Edison when she and the others had joined the depressed performers outside, at the ticket office.

'I don't think there's much she can do to save it,' he said. 'We've had it.'

'And I've had it, too,' snapped Wendy. 'You promised me that this circus would be successful again, and it isn't. So I'm off to join the Peck A. Daily Circus. At least *they* are successful.'

Sid didn't try to stop her as she marched towards her rusty old motor caravan. She had threatened to leave often enough before and he was sure this was just the latest threat.

'Just ignore her,' he said, confidently. 'She's always saying she'll leave, but she never does. She'll calm down.'

But this time she'd meant what she said. For just then her motor caravan started up, back-fired, revved up again and went shooting out of the show ground with a squeal of tyres.

'She's gone!' he cried. 'She's left me! Left Scouse's circus for ever! She must have meant it this time!'

'I'll go after her in *your* car,' Super Gran volunteered as she ran across the circus area ahead of the others. 'Where is it?' She looked round and spotted a rusty old

65

convertible with its top down, beside Sid's caravan. 'Ah, there it is . . .'

She ran to it, vaulted nimbly over the side without opening the door, and plopped down into the driver's seat. She switched on the ignition, put it into gear and the car moved slowly forward across the show ground – until one of its doors fell off and the windscreen washer decided to squirt water in her face.

'Jings! What's this?' she cried. 'Glug!'

Next, while the circus performers watched in amusement – and the children watched in amazement – she rose into the air, still sitting on the seat and still clutching the steering wheel!

'Crivvens, what's going on here?'

Her audience roared with laughter as the front wheels collapsed and the car nose-dived into the soil of the show ground.

'Jings! I'll no' get very far in this!' she murmured as the others went into hysterics. 'What tricky sort of car *is* this?'

'Tricky!' yelled Sid, between guffaws. 'That's just it! It's the circus trick car!'

'You might've told me,' she muttered as she climbed down from the airborne seat and jumped down out of the car.

'You didn't ask,' Walt laughed. 'You just went running on ahead of us.'

But the joviality didn't last long. Sid was soon wearing his sad face again.

'That's Wendy gone,' he said, 'and the circus will

never be the same again, now. She won't be here to nag me.'

At which Walt and Pepe, still wearing their parts of the pantomime horse skin, got together and, in an attempt at cheering him up, said:

'Don't worry, boss, *this* old nag . . .'

' . . . Will continue to nag you!'

Next day Super Gran gave Willard and Edison a lift on the electronic bike to the circus where they found Sid, Walt and Pepe moping around inside the Big Top looking extremely depressed. Having had to refund the entrance money and then having Wendy walk out on them, they felt they couldn't sink any lower.

'Cheer up,' Super Gran said, 'maybe you'll get an audience tonight.'

'Now, it's all washed up,' Sid moaned. 'We haven't sold any tickets for tonight – or any other night, for that matter!' He pointed round at the Big Top. 'And this is all in tatters. In fact, my *life's* all in tatters! We're finished.'

'I wish I could do something to help you,' she said, frowning. 'I could do some of your acts – in fact, I could do *all* of them! – that would be easy-peasy. But it wouldn't help you in the long run, would it? If only I could think of something else.'

Then her eye caught the words on a discarded poster which had been crumpled up and tossed into a corner of the Big Top.

'What's that – the Circus Championships?' she said as she smoothed out the paper to read it properly.

68

'Yeah, so what!' said Sid, without enthusiasm. 'That's no use to us. We haven't entered those for years now. We haven't been good enough.'

His eyes glazed over as he thought back to better days. 'I remember when we did enter, though. Yes, those were the days.' Then he came down to earth a bit. 'Mind you, we never won 'em, but at least we were good enough to take part.' Then he came *right* down to earth. 'Not that we'll ever be, again.' He sighed.

'It says here,' she went on, ignoring his self-pity, 'that they're being held this year at Paddleton. But that's just a few miles away.'

'Yeah,' he agreed. 'And they're on this week.'

'But anyone taking part in them has got to register today,' she went on, pointing to the poster. 'Before noon. So that doesn't give me much time, does it?'

'Time for what?' he asked, without much interest.

She tossed the poster aside and hurried towards the exit.

'Where are you going?' Edison asked.

'Yes, and time for what, Gran?' Willard added.

'To register this circus for the Championships!' she said, dropping her bombshell.

'What?' the three performers burst out. They couldn't believe their ears. Their mouths fell open. They were speechless.

'What?' Willard echoed. 'But ... but they're rubbish!'

Willard didn't mince his words. He just said what he thought!

'Hey! What d'you mean, rubbish?' retorted Sid, all insulted.

But before he and Willard could come to blows Edison asked:

'But how is this going to help Sid's circus, Super Gran?'

'If they could do well at the Championships,' she explained, 'then maybe they'll attract some star performers again. Then audiences will come and see them, and then they'll be successful once more.'

'Yeah,' Sid added, mournfully, 'and maybe Wendy will come back again.'

'Right,' she said, 'but I haven't time to stand here blethering. I've got to get along to Paddleton show ground to put your names down. And mine too.'

She looked at her watch. 'I've only got fifteen minutes to get there. I'm off.'

She rushed out of the Big Top, leapt on to the electronic bike and zoomed along the road to Paddleton.

8   Enter – Daily!

Ahead of Super Gran the Paddleton circus ground was crowded with would-be circus champions. Between fifty and sixty contestants were pushing, shoving and elbowing each other around at the ticket office outside the Big Top, while others tried to queue properly beside a notice which read: Circus Championships. Register your circus acts here.

'Hey! Gerroutofit!' barked Sharon Shuper, of Sharon's Shuper Shircus, to the fat lady from Terri Trooper's Troupe who poked her in the ribs in an attempt to get ahead of her in the queue.

'Ouch! Ooyah!' yelled the fat lady, as Sharon's handbag thumped her on the nose.

But the whole crowd was suddenly knocked aside by the arrival of the Peck A. Daily Circus, a rough bunch of circus louts led by Daily himself.

The Dailys were dressed in their usual circus clothes, their 'city gents' outfits. And Daily wore, in addition, his usual multi-coloured clown's face with its red nose and a large scarlet mop-like wig which peeked out from under his natty businessman's bowler hat.

'Move over, fatsos!' he commanded as his 'Dirty Dozen' pushed Sharon's Shircus out of their way.

In return he got a poke in the eye from a deadly weapon – Sharon's handbag!

71

'Here! Who ya shoving?' she asked.

'Ouch! I dunno! Tell me yer name and I'll tell you who I'm shoving!' he retorted as he and his horde continued to push until they reached the ticket office ahead of everyone.

'We're the Peck A. Daily Circus, from London,' he said, as he registered, 'and we're entering for – and gonna win! – the juggling, tight-rope walking, balancing, tumbling, clowning . . .'

After giving his performers' particulars to the woman in charge Daily looked round scornfully at the others.

'What're you lot doing here? You've got no chance in this contest. You've gotta be joking. You're just a bunch of circus sissies. You couldn't juggle a jigsaw puzzle! You couldn't balance a billiard ball! You couldn't walk a tight-rope if it lay on the ground! Go home to your Mummies and play with your dollies! Right? Right!'

And, to demonstrate his circus skills and prove just how good a performer he was, he pointed to the flagpole near the Big Top on which the Circus Championships flag was flying.

'See that? Want to see me run up it?'

'Go on, bet ya can't do it,' someone challenged him.

'Right. Watch this . . .'

He ran to the pole – and went straight up it!

It was amazing. And he hardly seemed to use his hands as he climbed. Or, if he did, he shot up the pole so quickly that no one noticed.

73

'Jings!' exclaimed Super Gran who arrived just then.

She was impressed as the others were, but Daily's climbing feat seemed to ring a bell with her. She vaguely recalled seeing something like it before.

She shook her head but the memory didn't come back to her, Super and all as she was. Maybe she had seen him performing in a circus? She didn't think so. She was sure it was in some other connection. Oh well, it probably didn't matter anyway.

She joined on at the back of the queue and eventually reached the ticket office.

'Whose circus are you registering?' she was asked.

'Sid Scouse's.'

On hearing this statement every contestant in the circus area roared with laughter.

'What're you laughing at?' she asked.

'Scouse's circus? Scouse's lousy!' retorted one of the performers who fancied himself as a bit of a poet.

'Yeah,' someone else said, 'he hasn't a hope in Helensburgh!'

'Oh, hasn't he?' Super Gran retorted, determinedly. 'Then maybe I should tell you that *I* am performing as part of his team, with some of my friends.'

She'd suddenly had the idea of roping in her friends Gladys, Mrs Preston, Postman Pugh and others to help Sid out. But Sid didn't know that, yet!

'What? You?' the contestants howled with laughter. 'A little old lady? You're terrifying us, missis!'

'Oh, didn't I tell you who I am? I'm Super Gran.'

Which got even more laughter from the circus performers who had never heard of her and her Super-powers. But she just smiled to herself, knowing they were in for surprises when she performed her circus acts.

But Daily didn't laugh along with the others. For not only had he heard of her and her Super-powers, he also recognized her – from a previous encounter.

He had spotted her from his position at the top of the flagpole and had almost fallen off, in shock, when she appeared at the ticket office below him. For he had an old score to settle with her.

His smile, beneath the clown's make-up, was replaced by an evil frown as he clutched the top of the pole.

'I'll have to deal with her and win the Championships at the same time,' he murmured.

Normally Scouse's Circus would have been no threat to him in winning this contest, but if Super Gran was in their team then that was a different matter. She might just possibly do enough by herself to pull them up to the standard of the other competitors. And this meant the odds against Daily were lengthening, and he didn't like that.

'Besides, there's only one way to win a contest,' he told himself, as he slid down the flagpole, 'and that is to cheat!'

But he and his Dailys would be too busy performing in – and winning! – the contest, to have time to do much cheating. So he would have to find someone else to do it for him.

75

'And that way no one will suspect me,' he thought. 'I'll have an alibi. I'll be somewhere else – on my way to the contest, or stuck in the traffic, while the job's being done.'

He reached the ground but had to push his way through the other performers who were gathered around, congratulating him on his pole run. He hadn't time for them, just then.

'But who shall I get?' he wondered. 'Who owes me a favour? Or who can I bully – or blackmail! – into doing it for me?'

It suddenly came to him. The very person!

'Of course – who else?'

He hurried away from the others, for privacy, then he opened a door in his clown's bowler hat, took out a cordless phone and dialled a number in Chisleton.

'Hello, Scunner? I've got a job for you . . . What's that, he's not in? When'll he be in? Not for twenty-five *years*? You mean minutes, don't you? You *don't*? You *mean* years? You sure? How come – he's not in Dartmoor, is he?'

The only person available to answer the phone in the Scunner's house was of course Tub, who had to explain that his uncle was now at R A F Paddleton.

'But that's just along the road,' Daily said. 'Ask him . . . correction . . . *tell* him to phone me. Right? Right!'

'But he isn't allowed to have phone calls,' said Tub. 'Not while he's doing basic training. And that lasts for weeks.'

'What?' Daily bellowed. 'But I can't wait for weeks.'

He paused and gave it some thought. 'Listen, get hold of his cordless phone and fetch it along to the camp. Then toss it over the fence to him so I can phone him. Gettit?'

'Y-yes . . .'Tub stuttered, nervously.

'Then do it!'

Daily snapped his phone back into its holster and thrust it inside his hat.

He grinned over at his Dailys and gave them the thumbs up sign. They were on their way to winning the contest and nothing could go wrong – Super Gran or no Super Gran.

9 Something Phone-y About This!

Tub found the Scunner's cordless phone and took it, by bus, to RAF Paddleton. But when he arrived there he had to hang about until he saw the recruits, being drilled, marching towards where he stood outside the fence that surrounded the camp.

'Pssst! Uncle!' he hissed as the squad of rookies marched past him, all at sixes and sevens as usual!

'Tub!'

The Scunner almost wept at the sight of him. Just to see someone from Chisleton wiped away a little bit of the loneliness. He was feeling homesick!

Admittedly he had the two Muscles with him but they didn't count! He still felt homesick even with them there!

'What're you doing here, Tub?' he called, as loudly as he dared, as the squad marched close to the fence.

'It's this, the phone . . . It's for you-hoo . . .!' Tub said as he lobbed it over the high wire towards him.

The Scunner now tried desperately to do three things at once. He tried to catch the flying instrument, he tried to retain hold of the rifle he was carrying and he tried not to let Flight Sergeant Brain, who was drilling them, see what was happening.

He didn't quite succeed! There was a loud clatter as he dropped his rifle to the ground.

'What's going on back there?' Brain roared, snapping his head round to scrutinize the rear of the squad. 'Ah, dropped your rifle have you, Campbell?' he gloated. 'That means a week's spud-bashing for you!'

The Scunner groaned at his punishment but was able at least to thrust the phone into his tunic, to hide it. But unfortunately Daily chose that precise moment to phone him!

'Prrr, prrr! Prrr, prrr!' went the phone. And:

'What's that? What's that?' went Brain when he heard it, his face turning scarlet at the very idea of one of his recruits having a telephone on his person. 'Is that a phone I hear?'

'No ... ah ... um ... it's just a dicky-bird,' the Scunner blurted out.

Brain looked all around him as the 'Prrr, prrr-ing' continued. There wasn't a dicky-bird within a mile of them. In fact, there wasn't even a tree in sight in which a dicky-bird could be hiding.

But while Brain was mulling this over the Scunner was able to slip his hand inside his tunic and press the little button on the phone to silence its ringing. Then he sighed with relief, while Brain scratched his head in bewilderment.

Later, when the squad returned to the barracks at the end of their drill session, exhausted as usual, the Scunner pulled the phone out from under his tunic. It was only now he had time to wonder about the whole incident.

'Wot's the phone for?' Cedric asked him.

'How should *I* know!'

'Wot was Tub here with it for?' Cedric went on.

'How should I know that, either!'

'Yeah, and why were you making it go "prrr, prrr" on the parade ground?' asked Dustin, stupidly. 'Huh?'

'It wasn't me making it go "prrr, prrr", you idiot,' the Scunner said. 'It was going "prrr, prrr" all by itself!'

Suddenly: 'Prrr-prrr . . . prrr-prr . . .' it went again.

And it happened so unexpectedly that he dropped the instrument to the floor as if it were red hot. 'Yeeks!'

'Hello . . . Hello . . .' said a voice from the floor.

He picked it up. 'Hello?'

'Is that the Rising Sun Chinese Restaurant?' a woman caller asked, politely.

'Sorry, madam, you've got the wrong number,' he said.

'I *know* it's a Wong number. I *want* a Wong number. I want Mr Wong of the Rising Sun Chinese Restaurant! I told you! *Is* that the Rising Sun Chine . . .?'

'No, madam, it most definitely is not,' he snapped as he slammed the receiver back into its holster.

Then he dialled his own number.

'Who ya phoning, boss?' Cedric asked him.

'I'm phoning Tub to ask him what this is all about and why he brought it in the first place. *Somebody* must want to call me.'

But Tub wasn't at home. He tried again later but he still wasn't at home.

He had no way of knowing, of course, that it was his old friend – and enemy! – Peck A. Daily who wanted to call him. So the only way he could find out was to wait until the phone rang again.

'Just as long as it doesn't ring on the parade ground,' he muttered. 'That's all.'

Later, after lunch, he was sitting alone on a stool behind the mess hut and he was sobbing bitterly.

But he wasn't sobbing because he hadn't got his phone call; he wasn't sobbing because he hadn't yet been given his Spitfire; he wasn't sobbing because he'd been given the potato-peeling duty as punishment for dropping his rifle on parade; and he wasn't sobbing because he had already peeled five sacks of the rotten things! He was sobbing because he was now peeling three pails of onions!

'What I want to know is, what am I messing about with all this for, anyway?' he muttered. 'I only joined this mob to be a fighter-pilot, like Pinky Attenborough.'

And just then Brain appeared, to nag him.

'Aren't you finished, yet, Campbell?'

'I'm finished, all right,' he retorted, through his teeth – and through his onion tears! 'I've had enough of all this. I want to quit – retire – you old curry-brain . . .'

'What's that?' Brain thundered. 'Quit? Retire? Curry-brain?'

'No . . . er . . . I said . . . um . . . ah . . . when shall I get my Spitfire . . . ah . . . or an old Hurricane?'

'Oh, is that what you said?' Brain said, not believing a word of it. But then a wicked gleam came into his eye. 'Look here, Campbell, you want to be a pilot, don't you?'

'I certainly do.' The Scunner's eyes lit up, expectantly. He would grovel at Brain's feet, if necessary, if it would get him his very own plane.

'Yes,' smirked Brain, 'I thought so.'

The Scunner threw away his vegetable knife with a joyful cry.

'I knew it. I knew I wouldn't have to peel spuds and onions for long. Pinky Attenborough never had to peel spuds and onions at all, you know!'

Brain then unexpectedly picked up a large shovel which was leaning against a wall, and handed it to him.

'See that over there?' He pointed to a lorry loaded with coal which had recently been delivered for the boiler-house.

'Yes?' The Scunner was puzzled. What had this to do with him being a pilot, he wondered.

'Take the shovel,' Brain instructed, 'remove the coal from the lorry and pile it in that heap over there. Pile it . . . pilot . . . Get it? Good, eh?'

And he laughed uproariously as the Scunner angrily threw the shovel down.

'It's an old gag, but the old 'uns are the best 'uns!' he guffawed as he turned on his heel and marched off.

The Scunner picked up his knife and resumed peeling the onions, over which his tears flowed. Only this time it wasn't just the onions which caused the tears, it was the sheer frustration he felt in being a prisoner at RAF Paddleton against his will, and without even a Spitfire to console him.

'That's it,' he muttered, throwing the knife down again. 'I've had enough. I'm going to escape – just as soon as I can.'

10   Tub, on his Own

Super Gran returned to Chisleton to join Sid, Walt, Pepe and the children to give them the news that she had entered Sid's circus for the Championships.

'They actually let you put our names down?' Sid exclaimed. 'With all the best circus performers in the country?'

She nodded and smiled, pleased with herself.

'But there are only the three of us,' he pointed out. 'And Walt's got his injured foot, too.'

'Jings, you forgot about me!' she cried indignantly.

'Yeah, that's true,' he admitted, thoughtfully. 'But I can't see you, me, Pepe and Walt – the way *he* is – putting up much of a show. And we don't even have Wendy, now. She'll be competing in Daily's Circus.' He sighed.

He missed her. And he missed being nagged!

But Super Gran tried to console him.

'I've got lots of friends who'll rally round and help us. In fact, I've actually entered *their* names for the competition, too.'

His eyes lit up. 'You have? Are they circus performers? Why didn't you tell me before?'

She hesitated. 'We-ell, they're not exactly performers. But I'm sure they could be taught some circus acts in time to perform in the contest . . .'

'What? You mean – they're amateurs?' he yelled, insulted.

'Aye, we-ell, I suppose so,' she admitted. 'But I'm sure with a wee bit of tuition . . . well, er . . . with a *lot* of tuition from you and Walt and Pepe they'll learn a few acts. We've still got a few days yet, and . . .'

'A few *days*!' cried the indignant Sid. 'It takes *years* to train circus performers, not *days*.'

'But I saw a programme on the telly where they taught people to do circus stunts in a week. From scratch,' she insisted.

'Scratch?' he howled. 'They'll be covered in scratches, and bruises, and bumps, by the time they're finished!'

'So you'll do it,' she smiled, taking that as a 'yes'. 'And remember, it'll only take a wee while to teach me, 'cos I'm a Super-quick learner. You saw how easily I learned to walk the ball and the tight-rope and the stilts. Then I'll help you and the others to train my friends. We'll do it. Honestly. Don't worry.'

She put on her most brilliant, confident smile, inspiring Sid to have as much confidence in her as she had in herself. So he eventually nodded his head, gave in and agreed.

'Oh, well, all right. We can only try,' he said. 'Things couldn't be any worse than they are now, that's for sure.'

'Aye, that's right,' she grinned, 'what've you got to lose?'

'Just my circus, that's all!' he snorted. 'But what are these friends of yours going to do? What acts are they hoping to learn?'

'Well,' she said, 'Gladys, I'm sure, is just dying to be fired out of a gun as a human cannonball.'

But Edison giggled at this. 'Oh, Super Gran, you shouldn't have said "dying"!'

Sid shook his head. 'She can't. We can't afford a cannon.'

'Well she can do something else,' Super Gran agreed. 'And Mrs Preston, I'm sure, would like to be a fire-eater – so long as it doesn't give her heart-burn! And Postman Pugh could juggle with the parcels from his post-bag – he's always doing that anyway, as he goes on his rounds, so that should be easy-peasy for him. And then, of course, there's your star turn – me!'

Sid laughed at her lack of modesty. 'And what are you going to do?'

'I'll have a go at everything,' she replied. 'But I'd really like to have a wee go on the trapeze. I've always fancied trying the flying trapeze.'

'But . . . ah . . . um . . .,' he stammered, 'er . . . what about your age?'

'D'you mean I'm too young?' she asked, innocently.

'I mean you're too old!' he retorted.

'Havers, laddie, you're only as old or as young as you feel – and I feel as young as Willard and Edison, here.'

'And what about Willard and Edison?' he asked. 'Aren't they going to perform for us? Everybody else is, apparently!'

'Jings, no,' she said. 'They're too young. They'll just sit in the audience with Inventor Black and watch the star of the show – me! – and you others, of course.'

'Aw, Gran,' Willard moaned, 'why can't I have a go at something?'

'You can.'

'I can?' His eyes lit up.

'Aye. You can have a go at rounding up Mrs Preston and Gladys and Postman Pugh and . . .'

'Huh, is that all!' he groaned. 'Why do *I* never get joining in the fun?'

'Because you're too wee, that's why.'

And so, for the next few days, Sid tried his best, with some help from Walt, Pepe and Super Gran, to train Mrs Preston and the others in attaining some circus skills – but without much success.

They tried out Gladys on the trampoline but she failed miserably.

'Help,' she cried, 'all that bouncing through the air makes me airsick.'

Mrs Preston wouldn't consider the idea of fire-eating but tried the plate-spinning act instead. But after she had dropped dozens of plates Sid protested.

'She's having a smashing time! But I can't afford all this broken crockery. She'll have to try a less expensive act!'

Pugh kept dropping his juggled parcels but didn't worry about it, even when the ones marked 'fragile' broke into pieces.

'I'm always smashing parcels marked "fragile", at work!'

And while the would-be circus artistes were practising in the circus, Willard and Edison were meeting a despondent Tub in town.

He envied the exciting life his uncle and the Muscles were leading – flying Spitfires, he thought – and he felt he was missing out on something. He was! But he didn't realize he was actually having the best of it!

'Huh! I bet he thinks it's his birthday getting into the air force and getting a plane,' he had murmured, then added: 'Hey! It *is* his birthday, soon.'

So that stopped his brooding and gave him something to think about.

He headed for his local newsagent's to buy a card. And he chose this particular shop because it sold not only newspapers and birthday cards but also ice cream!

'Well, I deserve one,' he murmured, 'seeing I wasn't allowed to get joining the air force. Huh!' He sighed.

And it was just then, outside the newsagent's, that he encountered Willard and Edison.

'Are you still missing your Uncle Scunner?' Edison asked him.

'Yeah,' he said, scuffing his feet aimlessly on the pavement. 'I've got nothing to do now he's not around.'

'Aw, that's a shame,' Willard said. But then spoiled his apparent sympathy by sniggering.

'And it's all right for him,' Tub went on, 'he's got what he wanted – flying Spitfires and Hurricanes. He's mad about Spitfires and Hurricanes.'

He left them and entered the shop where he grabbed the first birthday card he spotted. He spent two seconds choosing it, but took much longer to choose an ice cream cone for himself!

Super Gran met the children outside the shop as they continued to laugh at Tub's misery.

'Och, I'm sorry for the wee bachle,' she said. 'After all, he's all alone in the world, without his uncle and friends – even if they're all rotten wee poultices.'

'I'll bet even you are missing the Scunner are you not, Super Gran?' Edison asked.

'Blethers, lassie, I'm too busy in the circus to miss him,' she said. 'And I'm sure he's not missing me, or his old life here. He'll be having a great time of it, flying all over the sky in all those supersonic aeroplanes.'

'No, it's Spitfires and Hurricanes he's mad on,' Willard pointed out.

'Well, whatever they are. But what I mean is, he's enjoying himself so much he'll never want to come back to boring old Chisleton again.'

She entered the shop and collected her weekly magazines, *Grannies' Own* and *Grannies' Realm*. Then she spotted Tub.

'Hello, Tub. Is that a birthday card you're buying?'

He nodded silently, his mouth being too busy licking the ice cream to answer her.

'Who's it for?' she asked. 'Anyone I know?'

'Yeah, Uncle Scunner,' he told her, between slurps. 'His birthday's soon.'

'Oh, is it? Then I'll buy him a card too.'

She chose one from the card rack. On the front it read: 'You're twenty-one – for the umpteenth time!'

'Will this do?' she asked, but he just shrugged.

She opened it and read the verse out, aloud:

'To those we miss the most we say, happy returns on your special day.'

She handed her money to the shop assistant and as she and Tub left the shop together, Tub sighed.

'Are you missing him?' she asked and he nodded, miserably.

'Yeah,' he muttered, with a faraway look in his eye. 'I'm stuck here at home while Uncle Scunner and the others are enjoying themselves in the air force. It's not fair.'

He sighed again and – incredibly! – dropped his unfinished ice cream cone into a waste-paper bin. He really *was* distracted!

They parted company at the corner. Tub carried on along the High Street to go off and continue with his boring, meaningless life, his hands in his pockets and his shoulders hunched, while Super Gran joined Willard and Edison again.

'The poor wee soul's all depressed,' she explained. 'Just because the Scunner and those two other wee bachles were taken into the RAF, and he wasn't. I feel sorry for the wee midden.'

'And it's funny not having the Scunner around creating trouble every day, isn't it?' Edison said.

'There's no crime being committed,' Willard added. 'Everything's peaceful and quiet. Nothing's happening ...'

'Yes – boring, isn't it!' Super Gran and Edison said, together, and laughed.

11   How to HANDLE Hangars – and Helicopters!

The Scunner, the Muscles and the other recruits were having a few precious moments of peace as they rested on their beds in the hut – to recover from Brain-damage!

Suddenly the Scunner's phone rang.

'Hello, is that you, Scunner? At last! This is Peck A. Daily. Why didn't you answer, before? Huh? I've phoned you about five times already. I seem to have been calling you, daily.'

'Oh, so it's you who's been calling, is it?' he rasped. 'Well, I'd like to be able to speak to you, Daily – daily! – but I'm in the air force now, you know. Doing basic training. And not allowed too many phone calls, as you can appreciate!'

'Yeah, yeah, yeah, never mind all that. I don't want a sob story, do I? What I want is for you to get over here right away, to the Paddleton show ground. I need your help at the Circus Championships . . .'

'I'm deeply flattered, Daily, but I'm not exactly an accomplished acrobat, you know!'

'Not that kinda help,' Daily said. 'I've got a little job for you. Right? Right!'

'I'd be delighted to help you,' the Scunner lied, 'but

you'll have to wait twenty-five years, till I'm demobbed!'

'Yeah, I heard all about that, but I can't wait that long. I need you in a couple of days' time.'

'We're due some leave in about six weeks, I believe!' The Scunner was trying to be helpful.

'Look, Campbell,' said Daily, his voice hardening. The pleasant niceties were over and he wasn't going to be messed about any longer. 'You'll come over here and see me, even if you've got to cut the wire and escape. Or dig a tunnel. Or build a wooden horse or whatever you've gotta do. Gettit? Or else . . .'

'Or else what . . .?' demanded the Scunner, toughly. He wasn't going to be pushed around by the likes of him.

'Or else I'll tell the police about a certain job you and your men pulled in Chisleton's big store, Chizbury's, last month.'

'Oh, all right, you win,' grumbled the Scunner, defeated. And besides, he wanted to escape anyway.

'You know where to come,' Daily said, 'the show ground.'

'Yes, yes,' he snapped, slamming the phone's handset back into its holster, cutting Daily off.

'Are you gonna escape, to meet him?' Cedric asked, when the Scunner had repeated the conversation.

'I'm escaping all right,' he said, with determination, 'but I'm not going anywhere near that nutcase. I'm going straight . . .'

'You're going straight, boss?' Cedric was shocked. 'You're giving up crime?'

'I'm going straight,' he went on, after the interruption, 'home – to ma ain wee hoose in Chisleton!'

And next morning he thought his prayers were answered when Brain announced: 'Today, you're leaving Paddleton . . .'

'Oh goodie, free at last! Chisleton here I come!'

'. . . To go to RAF Wallytown,' Brain continued, finishing his sentence. 'Where you'll get a whole day's experience of a real, actual air force station – as opposed to Paddleton, which is only a Mickey Mouse one, a mere training camp. Come on now, hup, two, three, four! Let's be having you – into your private transport . . .'

'Oh no, not that rotten old heap again,' the Scunner moaned, as they climbed into three RAF lorries that were waiting to take them the few miles along the road to the airfield.

'Well at least we'll see some Spitfires and Hurricanes,' Cedric pointed out.

The Scunner brightened. 'You're right, there is that.'

'And those Soppy Camels, too,' Dustin added, smiling inanely.

And certainly the first things they saw, on entering RAF Wallytown, were a number of huge aircraft hangars.

'Right,' said Brain when they had jumped from the lorries, 'the first thing you've got to learn is how to open the hangar doors. This one'll do.' They stopped at the first hangar they reached.

'Wow! They're some height,' murmured Dustin, looking up at the huge, high doors which towered above them.

'Right,' Brain yelled, 'let's be having you. Two-six on the hangar doors!'

'What does he mean?' the Scunner asked one of the others.

But while the recruit was shrugging that he didn't know, Brain was yelling an explanation: 'I mean, get those hangar doors open – at the double. Quick! Chop, chop! Get on with it!'

'But what do we open them with?' the Scunner asked. 'They're gigantic. It would take someone as strong as . . . As strong as . . .'

He couldn't bring himself to say her name.

'As strong as Super Gran, he means!' Dustin prompted, in his gormless way.

Dustin had no scruples about mentioning Super Gran's name, whereas his boss thought the sky would fall on him if he uttered it out loud!

'Yeah, well, as strong as S-Super Gran,' he admitted. '*We* couldn't open it. Not unless we all had a go at it,' he added, looking round at the other recruits.

'There's no need for that, Campbell,' Brain explained as he emerged, with a large handle, from a small shed attached to the hangar.

'Hey,' the Scunner yelled, 'that looks like the handles they used in the old days to start cars with.'

'Right!' Brain pounced. 'So if you know all about it, you can show the others how to open the hangar doors with it!'

'But . . . but . . .' the Scunner protested, in vain.

Brain pushed the handle into the slot in the door and then turned it a couple of revolutions, to demonstrate how easily it opened once the handle was employed.

'See? It's easy. Even you could do it,' he said, gesturing to the Scunner that it was now his turn to turn the handle.

At first everything went smoothly but after he had turned it a few times the handle's momentum caused it to revolve on its own, without his help.

'Let it go now, Campbell,' Brain warned, 'and stand back! Otherwise it'll whirl round and catch you, and . . . Oh-oh . . . Oh, dearie me, what's happened?' he said, pretending concern.

'Ouch! Ooyah! Help!' yelled the Scunner.

'Hey, Dustin, the boss can't handle the handle!' joked Cedric as the object, whirling round it seemed at the speed of sound, caught the Scunner in the stomach and threw him metres away, to land on his back.

He lay there battered, bruised and bewildered. Then he cursed the handle, the hangar doors, Brain, the air force – and everyone else he could think of! Including Super Gran!

'Oh, get up, stop snivelling and pull yourself together,' Brain ordered, as he grabbed him by the collar and yanked him to his feet.

But he was winded and sore, and bent over as he

clutched his injured stomach. He wished, heartily, that he was back again in good old Chisleton, away from this dangerous R A F he had talked himself into joining. And away from this Brain whose whining voice was starting to drill a hole in *his* brain!

But worse was to follow!

Now that the hangar doors had been opened the recruits could see the large helicopter which stood inside.

'Right,' Brain said, 'your next job is to get that chopper out of there and on to the apron outside. Savvy?'

'What . . . what with?' asked the Scunner, gasping through his pain. 'Haven't you . . . got tractors . . . in the air force . . . for doing things like . . . that . . .?'

'Of course,' Brain smirked, 'but that's the easy way. And we don't want to make it too easy for you, now do we?'

'Y E S!' yelled all the recruits, in unison, at the top of their voices, but Brain ignored them.

'Come on, two-six on the helicopter,' he yelled, by way of encouragement, 'let's be having you. Push! Push! Push!'

And it was then that the Scunner made two mistakes. First of all, in order to push the helicopter he positioned himself right in front of one of its fat, heavy little wheels. And secondly, he decided he had done enough work for one day.

'Huh,' he muttered, looking round and counting the recruits, 'there's plenty of others pushing this thing. They can manage without me.'

So he stopped pushing. But he forgot to step to the side, out of the way of the fat, heavy little wheel which was still moving behind him! The helicopter trundled forward – and knocked down the skiving Scunner!

'Ow! Ouch! Ooyah! Help! Get me up!' he yelled, in agony, as the wheel ran right over the back of his leg and pinned him to the ground.

'Trust you, Campbell!' Brain yelled as the recruits and the Muscles used their muscles to reverse the helicopter away from him, to enable his leg to be hauled out from under its wheel.

'Ow-ow-ow!' he cried.

'Idiot!' Brain barked, showing him no sympathy whatsoever.

He was carried by his fellow recruits to a bench, inside the hangar, where he sat and tried to massage some feeling back into his leg again. Then, when he had recovered slightly, he said:

'I'll bet I'm the only man in the RAF who's ever been run over by a helicopter, eh, chief?'

He looked up at Brain as he spoke and put on a brave smile which fooled no one, let alone Brain.

'I wouldn't bet on it!' he retorted, bringing him down to earth again. 'It happened to that author chap. You know, the one who writes all those books about that little old Super Gran lady. Whatsisname? Well, anyway, he was run over by an RAF chopper, apparently.'

But the Scunner wasn't interested in authors. He was too busy cursing everyone in sight.

'Curses!' he cursed. 'Curse that hangar door and curse that chopper. I'd like to take a chopper to the chopper!'

'It's just as well you've got fat legs, though, eh, boss?' Cedric pointed out. 'Otherwise you'd've been injured.'

'I *am* injured, you buffoon,' he retorted. 'First my stomach on that flippin' flipping hangar handle, and now my leg on this hel . . . hel . . .'

'Language, boss!' said Dustin, smiling his gormless smile.

'Hel . . . hel . . . helicopter!' the Scunner continued.

Brain shook his head at his recruit's stupidity and walked out of the hangar, yelling to the others as he went:

'Right, lads. Back to the chopper. Let's be having you. Move, move. Chop chop on the chopper! And you too, Campbell.'

The Scunner watched him go. Then he got on to his feet and, with a little help from the Muscles, limped out of the hangar. But he didn't follow Brain. He headed in a different direction altogether!

'Right! That does it!' he decided. 'I've had it! I've had enough of this RAF lark. I'm definitely going to escape – as soon as possible. Just see if I don't!'

12   This Chapter is Full of Escapism!

As soon as they returned to the barrack hut the Scunner dived on to his knees and began to prise up one of the floorboards, with his rifle bayonet. He was going to tunnel his way out of Paddleton!

'Why didn't I think of this before?' he yelled as everyone in the hut watched him with open-mouthed amazement. 'This is the only way out of here,' he burbled.

'What's the big Scottish haggis up to, now?' one of the recruits muttered.

Had the Scunner finally flipped his lid?

'No problem,' he informed the Muscles, who stared down at him, as puzzled by his behaviour as the others. 'I've seen lots of those old escape films at the cinema and loads of episodes of *Colditz* on TV. I know enough about escaping to be able to get out of here without any bother! See?'

'Are you sure, boss?' Cedric asked him, doubtfully.

'It won't take long, lads, and then – I'll be free, free . . .!'

He finally raised the floorboard and he sat back on his heels, triumphantly.

But suddenly a number of men dressed in RAF uniforms popped their heads up out of the opening.

'Hello, mate,' one of them greeted him. 'Are we outside, yet? Have we made it? Have we escaped at last?'

'Huh? Who are you?' asked the dumbfounded Scunner, who couldn't believe his eyes.

'We're recruits from a previous intake,' the man said, 'and we've been trying for *years* to escape from Paddleton! We've been wandering about down here since 1975! Cor! It ain't half dark!'

The Scunner slammed the floorboard down and hammered it into place with his rifle butt.

'Yeeks! Pinky Attenborough never found other people wandering about in *his* escape tunnel,' he muttered. 'Why is nothing going right for me? Eh?'

'Huh? What's up, boss?' Cedric asked him. 'Looks like you've seen a ghost, or summat.'

The truth was that the Scunner was now so exhausted and confused that he had only imagined he had seen the would-be escapers. Or had he . . .?

'What are we going to do with them? Sid Scouse asked Walt and Pepe in desperation.

He pointed to Super Gran's amateur circus performers who were scattered around the Big Top practising their circus skills – or rather, their lack of circus skills!

It was now a couple of days before the contest was due to take place and Sid looked really worried. The thought that these friends of Super Gran were supposed to be representing him and his circus didn't bear thinking about. They were a motley crew and all the tuition in the world would never improve them. They simply had no talent for circus work.

'They're hopeless!' He shook his head.

'We'd have a better chance on our own,' Walt said. 'Just you and Pepe – and me with my bad foot and eye!'

'You're right,' Sid agreed, 'plus Super Gran, of course.'

Then he winced as Postman Pugh, the would-be stilt-walker, fell off them for the hundredth time!

'We won't get past the first round with that lot,' said Pepe.

'We won't get *into* the first round!' Walt retorted.

'No, it won't do,' Sid murmured, trying not to let Super Gran's friends hear him.

He didn't want to disappoint them. They had tried hard to learn and it wasn't their fault. He, Walt and Pepe – bad as they were, nowadays – would have a better chance on their own, with Super Gran.

This made him wonder where she was. She'd had another of her sudden ideas and zoomed off somewhere on her electronic bike, an hour ago.

But just then she returned, in her usual dramatic fashion.

Beaming broadly she whizzed through the entrance, steered the bike towards the centre of the ring and leapt off. The bike careered onwards and skidded in a nose-dive into the sawdust, where it 'putt-putted' to a halt.

'Where've you been?' he asked.

'To Paddleton. To the circus. Talking to some of the star contestants. Persuading them to join *us*, in the contest.'

Her huge grin indicated just how pleased she was with herself.

'Stars? Performing for me?' He couldn't believe it. He smiled but then he frowned again. 'But how can they? Aren't they performing for their own circuses?' He couldn't understand it.

'Aye, but don't worry, it's allowed. It's not against the rules. I checked. They can perform with two circuses if they want to, see? No problem. And this should give you a real chance, especially against the Peck A. Daily circus. 'Cos Daily, they say, wants to beat you, for old times' sake!'

'But how did you manage to get the stars to work for me?' he asked.

'Easy-peasy. I just spoke to the ones who worked for you before Daily pinched them. And persuaded them they should work for you now, seeing how good you were to them in the old days.'

'But not the ones in Daily's circus, surely?'

'Jings, no! I didn't go near them. Just the ones who've left him and are working for other circuses. No, none of Daily's mob would work for you. No way.'

'Well, that's great, Super Gran.' He grinned happily.

'And . . . er . . . um . . . I also promised them,' she went on, hesitantly, 'that you'd . . . um . . . pay them for doing it!'

'What?' he stormed. 'How am I going to get money to pay them? You know I'm broke. I haven't even got three pound coins to juggle with, never mind pay a lot of circus stars.'

'Don't worry,' she explained, 'once they've helped you win the contest the audiences will flock back to your shows. Then you'll get the money to pay the stars and to buy a new Big Top and other things, and you'll be able to hire other star performers for *all* your shows. See?'

Sid brightened. She seemed to have thought of everything.

'And this means we'll really have a chance in the competition.'

'We might even get past the first round,' Pepe said.

'And we can get rid of that lot!' Walt said, loudly, as he pointed to Super Gran's friends.

'Shhhhh!' Sid put his finger to his lips.

Now he wouldn't have to call on them after all, which was a relief, but he didn't want to offend them, or Super Gran. They had meant well.

'Don't worry,' Super Gran smiled, as she went over to Postman Pugh and the others, 'I'll tell them the bad news. But I'll break it to them gently that they're no longer required!'

But, thought Sid sadly, I am going to have to break it to you, Super Gran, that you are no longer required, either . . .!

The next day, just as the recruits were leaving their

hut to report for yet another drill session, the Scunner's phone rang.

'Are you still at that camp, Campbell?' Daily barked angrily. 'I thought I told you to get over here right away?'

'Yes, well ... ah ... um ...' he stammered. 'I haven't ... er ... managed to ... um ... escape yet, you see, and ...'

But Daily interrupted him.

'Look, Campbell, you'd better get out of there today! Or else! And I won't tell you again! Right? Right!'

'But ...'

'Listen, I'll make it easier for you. I'm going to be in Chisleton this afternoon. I'll meet you at your house. Gettit?'

And he rang off before the Scunner could argue with him. So he had no option now. He simply had to escape, somehow. Today! Which didn't give him much time to dig a tunnel!

'Come on, move yourself, move yourself!' barked Brain, suddenly zooming into the hut to haul him on to the parade ground. 'What are you hanging about in here for? Jump to it!'

He'd just had time to thrust the phone under his pillow before Brain spotted it.

Then, when they joined the others outside, Brain announced:

'Concorde is due to fly over RAF Paddleton, this morning.'

The recruits cheered, in unison.

'But it doesn't mean,' he went on, 'that you, Campbell, and the rest of you rotten rookies are going to get away with any of your usual drill, so don't think it! See?'

The recruits groaned, in unison.

'I've gotta escape!' the Scunner muttered to his men as they marched alongside him, back and forward across the parade ground.

But the Muscles were not paying attention to him. For they were too busy *not* paying attention to their marching and were, as usual, bumping into the other recruits and were turning to their right instead of to their left, and so on.

'Hup, two, three, four,' Brain yelled at the undisciplined squad. 'Left, right, left, right . . .'

And it was just then, in the middle of their drill session, that Concorde flew over and gave the Scunner the chance he'd been waiting for – the chance to escape!

13 The Great Escape!

As Brain and the recruits marched past the main gate they gazed upwards as Concorde flew over. And so did the guards, who had emerged from the guardroom especially to see it.

So the Scunner – the only person at RAF Paddleton not looking skywards! – took his chance. He veered to the right, away from the squad, and marched quickly towards the gate, past the guards – to freedom. And Flight Sergeant Brain never noticed!

'Left wheel!' he yelled and the squad, still looking upwards, wheeled left, which took them even farther away from the escaping Scunner. 'Left, right, left, right . . .'

As he marched through the open gateway he glanced back at the parade ground and waved a not-so-fond farewell to it.

'Goodbye, mugs,' he rasped quietly, in case one of the guards heard him and hauled him back again!

He marched away from the camp along the road to dear old Chisleton and as he went he said, with feeling:

'And good riddance to the lot of you! And you too, Pinky Attenborough! If that's the best you can do – a rotten air force without Spitfires, Hurricanes and

Sopwith Camels – then you can keep it! It's not what I thought it was.'

'Left, right, left, right . . .' Brain continued inside the camp. 'Hey! Wait a minute . . . One, two, three, four . . .'

He stopped to count the marching recruits and discovered he was one short. One of them was missing!

'Campbell! Where's Campbell?'

The missing recruit passed a signpost which read 'good old Chisleton – a bit farther' at which he smiled contentedly. Then he passed another sign which read 'good old Chisleton – not far now' at which he smiled even more contentedly.

'Well, Scunner, you haven't far to go now to your ain wee hoose! Great, eh?'

And, tired as he was, he leapt in the air joyfully and clicked his heels together.

Then he came back down to earth, frowned and muttered: 'But I wonder what Daily wants me for?'

Presently he reached Chisleton where he yelled at the top of his voice: 'I'm home! The Scunner Campbell's home!' breaking into a run towards the High Street. Which made a change from him breaking into a bank in the High Street!

But his triumphant yell had been heard by Super Gran who was having a go at unicycling and was showing off her skills to Willard and Edison in the circus area.

'What was that?' she asked, putting her hand to her ear to help her Super-hearing. 'Oh, so the Scunner's returned, has he?'

'That'll be an end to the peace and quiet then, eh, Gran?' Willard said.

'Or maybe he's just paying us a "flying" visit,' joked Edison.

'Well at least it solves a wee problem for me.'

Her eyes twinkled as she jumped off the unicycle.

'What problem?' Willard asked.

'His birthday card. I forgot to ask Tub which camp he was stationed at. But it doesn't matter if he's back home. I've just got to deliver it, now.'

As she said this she pulled a creased envelope containing the card from her cardigan pocket and she smoothed out some of its wrinkles. It was addressed to 'Scunner Campbell'.

'You've got it with you?' Edison said, surprised.

'Aye, I've been carrying it about with me since I bought it. But I won't even have to post it to his house, now.'

'What d'you mean, Gran?' Willard asked.

'I'll show you.'

She held it out at the full stretch of her arm and, closing one eye, she squinted over the top of it, aiming at where she'd heard the Scunner's voice. Then after pulling her arm back to her face she flicked it forward again and threw the envelope, like a frisbee, with her full Super-strength.

It whooshed through the air, then seconds later:

'Ouch! What the . . .?' exclaimed the Scunner as the flying card knocked the beret off his head and landed at his feet.

He stopped to pick them both up.

'I've heard of "air mail",' he murmured, 'but that was ridiculous! And there's no stamp on it. I'll bet it's from that mean old bat, Super Gran. Aye, it is, I thought so.'

But Super Gran wasn't the only one who was thinking about the Scunner, for back at RAF Paddleton Flight Sergeant Brain was also thinking about him. In fact, he was screaming at the guards:

'Where's that cretinous creep Campbell got to? Search the entire camp. Search every cranny and nook for that rotten crook. Search his hut. Search under his hut! Search every inch of the camp. Search all the escape tunnels! Search Concorde ... naw, even he couldn't have escaped that way, could he . . .?'

But when the guards reported back to him twenty minutes later, they had to confess failure in finding any trace of him.

'He's escaped, I know it,' Brain said, 'but not for long. I'll get him back or my name isn't Pinky Attenborough!'

He stopped, realizing what he'd said.

'See? Now he's got me believing *I*'m Pinky Attenborough!'

But he pulled himself together and yelled:

'Fetch a jeep. I'm going after that deserter. And when I catch him he'll get his deserts all right!'

Then when the jeep and driver arrived he commandeered a sergeant and a corporal to accompany them in case the Scunner put up a struggle. Presently the vehicle was roaring out through the gates with Brain standing in the passenger's seat scrutinizing the countryside all around with a pair of powerful binoculars, like a laser beam sweeping a rock concert.

'Head for Chisleton,' he said.

And as soon as Brain had left, Cedric urged Dustin: 'Come on!' He grabbed his arm. 'Now's our chance. Let's go . . .' And he ran towards the perimeter fence.

'Where to?' asked Dustin, looking all round and blinking stupidly as he watched his mate run.

Cedric dived at the fence and crawled under it to reach the road outside – and freedom! Dustin eventually followed him.

'We'll soon reach Chisleton,' yelled Cedric, running to the right – towards Chisleton.

'Yeah, we'll soon reach Chisleton,' yelled Dustin, running to the left – towards Paddleton!

Cedric had to run after him, and turn him round!

'We'll soon reach Chisleton,' smirked a determined Brain from where he stood, binoculars to his eyes, in the jeep. 'And then that conniving Campbell will get what's coming to him.'

Ahead of them the Scunner was crossing the football pitch in Chisleton Park towards his villa and was beaming at the sight of his home sweet home again. And he clutched Super Gran's card in his hand.

But he stopped, in horror, as he saw the RAF jeep screaming up the street and screeching to a halt outside his house. He was caught. Brain, his driver and the two NCOs leapt from the vehicle, advanced

on him threateningly, and surrounded him.

'We've got you, Campbell. You're a deserter, now,' Brain said, with a nasty smirk. 'Tut, tut, you naughty man. This will mean the glasshouse for you, for ten years, at least.'

'The glasshouse?' The Scunner was mystified. 'You mean, a hothouse? But I don't like gardening. So what would I do with a hothouse for ten years?'

'Hothouse? What're you talking about? The glasshouse, in the forces, is what you civilians call prison!'

'Prison?' The Scunner was horrified.

'Yes,' Brain gloated, 'and after you do your ten years in the glasshouse you'll come out and *then* you'll start doing your twenty-five years in the RAF.'

'What? But that's thirty-five years altogether,' he protested, demonstrating his mental arithmetic. 'But anyway,' he smirked, thinking he had outwitted the flight sergeant, 'I've retired from the RAF, now. I'll send you a letter about it tomorrow.'

But Brain's smirk out-smirked, and out-ranked, the Scunner's.

'In the first place, we don't use the word "retire" in connection with leaving the services. We use the word "resign" . . .'

'Oh, all right, then,' he interrupted, 'I've resigned. Is that better?'

'Not really,' Brain said. 'I was going on to say that you can't leave the forces, just like that. You'll have to buy yourself out . . .'

'Oh, all right, if you insist,' the Scunner said, fishing

in his tunic pockets and coming up with the grand sum of one pound thirty-seven pence.

'Huh!' Brain snorted. 'If that's all you've got it'll take you three hundred years to pay it up! You'd be out sooner just doing your thirty-five years!'

'What?' The Scunner was flabbergasted.

'There's nothing else for it. We're here to take you back to Paddleton. You've no option. There's no argument. But don't worry, you'll soon get to like it. It's just the basic training you won't like.' Then he smirked, rubbed his hands together in anticipation and added: 'And I can guarantee you won't like that, one little bit! Tee, hee, hee!'

The Scunner really was trapped this time, there was no way out for him. He bit his lip and almost burst into tears!

14 Super Gran to the Rescue

The Scunner glanced at the birthday card in his hand and he thought of a way out – and then he really did burst into tears! For doing what he was about to do was going to hurt his pride.

He opened his mouth and yelled in his loudest, most strident, rasping voice:

'Su-per Gran . . .! He-elp . . .! He-elp . . .! He-elp . . .!'

'Uh!' said the deafened Brain as he and the three deafened airmen covered their ears with their hands.

The Scunner looked upwards with a worried frown but then he relaxed and smiled. He had spoken her name out loud and the sky hadn't fallen on him after all!

And at the circus site Super Gran heard his cry for help with her Super-hearing, but could hardly believe her ears!

'Jings! That sounded like the Scunner's voice! But it couldn't be, could it? Calling on wee me for help? Crivven! Wonders will never cease!'

'You'd better go and see, Super Gran,' Edison advised.

'Right, then. Where's the electronic bike?'

Minutes later, after the bike went like the Super-clappers along the road to the Scunner's house, she was confronting Brain and his men. But by this time they were pushing the reluctant recruit into the jeep although he was resisting their efforts by fighting, biting and struggling every inch of the way.

'Get 'im in, men!' Brain yelled. 'Ouch! My eye!'

'Gerroffme! Ooyah!' yelled the Scunner.

'Scunner! What's going on? Are you being kidnapped?'

'Super Gran!' For the first time in his life he was glad to see her. 'They won't let me retire from the air force.'

'Resign!' Brain corrected.

'Well, resign,' he said. 'I've to buy myself out with a huge sum of money I can't afford. And I just want to stay here in my ain wee hoose!'

'Jings! It's more like *them* paying *you* a huge sum of money to get rid of you!' she laughed, at which the Scunner looked rather peeved.

But then she relented: 'Oh, all right, I'll help you . . .'

'What?' Brain couldn't believe it. '*You*'ll help him? That's a laugh! What can a weak little old lady do to help this runaway rookie?'

He soon found out!

She grabbed the four airmen in turn, hauled them away from the Scunner, lifted them off their feet and tossed them into the jeep. Then while they were still dazed, bruised and confused and lay in heaps in the vehicle she demonstrated her full Super-strength by pushing it and its passengers backwards out of the street. Then she dusted off her hands, with satisfaction.

But this had the opposite effect on Brain to the one intended. For instead of being mad at her he was pleased! Her feats had impressed him so much he jumped out of the jeep and ran back to her.

'That was fantastic, lady! You're strong!' he said.

'I'm *not* strong,' she denied indignantly, 'I'm Super-strong!'

She quickly listed a few of her other Super-powers and watched while his eyes opened wider and wider at each revelation.

Brain had now reached both of them but he pushed the Scunner aside disdainfully. *He* required too much training and was of no immediate use to the air force. But Super Gran was something else! She could be useful to the air force right now!

'Would you like to enlist in the SGS?' he asked eagerly, as he whipped an enlistment form out of his tunic pocket and waved it in her face. 'Go on, join up and help us. Pl-ease . . .?'

'What does "SGS" stand for?' she asked.

'It's the Special Granny Service! And you'd be a great asset to it. In fact I shouldn't be at all surprised if you didn't even get your very own personal helicopter.'

'A helicopter? All to myself?' She was thrilled to bits.

'What?' The indignant Scunner turned to Brain. 'She'd get her own helicopter? And you wouldn't give me a rotten old Spitfire? Humph! Favouritism! Teacher's pet!'

But Super Gran had a twinkle in her eye as she asked Brain:

'Is that enlistment form you're waving at me the same as the ones you used for the Scunner and his men?'

'Yes, lady, the very same.'

'No, I don't think it is,' she argued, frowning.

'It is, I can assure you.'

'No, I'm sure it's not,' she insisted.

'It is. Look, here they are . . .'

Not realizing he was falling into a trap, Brain pulled three completed forms from his pocket and waved them in the air.

'May I see them?' she asked, innocently.

What's the old battleaxe up to now? the Scunner wondered. He soon found out!

'Thanks!'

She grabbed the forms from Brain and, quick as a Super-flash, she tore them into tiny pieces, threw them into a large waste-paper bin at the edge of the kerb, and shook it around.

'Huh?' gasped Brain, taken aback. 'What're you doing? What have you done?'

He turned to the sergeant who had managed to untangle himself from the other two airmen in the jeep and now joined Brain.

'Sergeant, retrieve those forms. At once!'

'Yes, Flight,' he said and turned to the corporal who had managed to extricate himself from the jeep's driver and was hurrying towards them.

'Corporal, retrieve those forms. At the double!'

'Yes, Sarge,' he said and turned to the driver who had jumped out of the jeep and was ambling in their direction.

'Airman, retrieve those forms. Jump to it, move yourself, move yourself!'

'Do what?' said the airman. 'Put my hand into that dirty old waste bin for a zillion little pieces of paper that nobody could glue together again anyway? You've gotta be joking.'

'Airman! That's insubordination!' yelled Brain, the sergeant and the corporal in unison.

But the driver merely shrugged and walked back to the jeep.

'I'm just an ordinary, ignorant airman. I don't understand words like "insub-thingamy". So there!'

Super Gran and the Scunner had been silently watching this exchange between the various members of the air force but now she turned to him.

'Well, that's it, I suppose. I guess that's you and your men demobbed, Scunner.'

'Hey, whadya mean?' shouted Brain. 'They can't be demobbed.'

'Then you'll have to pull all the rubbish out of that bin, find all the wee bits of your enlistment forms and glue them all together again in the correct order.' She grinned hugely. 'And somehow I don't think you'll do it. And your men aren't too keen, either. So the Scunner's demobbed, isn't he?'

Just then the two Muscles came running across the park towards the Scunner's villa, arriving just in time to hear the good news of their demob.

126

'Oh, goody goody,' said Cedric. 'Does that mean we don't have any more drilling to do?'

'Not unless you want to become a dentist!' Super Gran joked.

'And we don't have to go back?' asked the gormless Dustin.

'No,' she assured him, 'the only ones who have to go back are these four wee bachles here.'

She turned to Brain. 'Come on, get on your bike. Or rather, get back in your jeep, creep!'

There was nothing else for it. Brain, the NCOs and the driver climbed reluctantly into their vehicle and drove off. And that was one battle the RAF had lost – the battle with Super Gran!

'Well, then,' she said, turning to the Scunner, 'now I've got time to speak to you, at last – welcome home, "Boggles, Air Ace"!'

'Huh, just call me Scunner Campbell, that's all I am, I'm no one else. I'm not Boggles and I'm not Pinky Attenborough. I'm only me, myself. And I've learned my lesson not to try to be someone I'm not.'

Then he added: 'I'm telling you, I'll never leave good old Chisleton again. Never!' And, full of emotion, he gave a sniff.

'Oh no!' Super Gran groaned. 'Jings, don't say that! I might have known there would be a snag in helping to get you demobbed!'

15 Nasty Nobblers!

On the day of the Circus Championships the eager contestants arrived at Paddleton show ground. And they arrived in every conceivable type of transport, travelling by car, caravan or truck. But Sid, Walt and Pepe travelled in their trick circus car as they intended using it in their act, although they made sure it didn't do any tricks on the way over! And attached to it was a trailer carrying all their pieces of equipment.

Super Gran, Willard, Edison and Inventor Black, in his wheelchair, arrived early to have a look round the Paddleton circus area, to compare it with the tatty Scouse one!

'Sid and the others seem to have arrived all right in their trick car,' Super Gran said.

'And look at those, Gran!' Willard said.

He was pointing to a number of trick bicycles which some of the clowns from the circuses had ridden there to catch the public's attention. And these bikes had crazy, wobbling wheels or saddles which rose and fell with every movement of the pedals.

'And those must be the dressing-rooms,' Edison pointed out as they strolled around the Big Top.

These were actually two smaller tents, separate ones for the men and the women, in which they would put on their costumes and make-up. And they were attached to the rear of the Big Top but had openings in them to give the performers access to the ring.

Super Gran and company now entered the Big Top to take their seats in the front row beside Mrs Preston, Gladys, Postman Pugh and the rest of their friends.

'What are those things?' Edison asked, pointing to the large boards attached to poles, at either end of the ring.

'That's the scoreboards, silly,' Willard told her. 'To mark each team's score up on when the contest starts.'

Sid emerged from the dressing-room, backstage, and crossed the ring to greet his supporters.

'Why aren't you getting ready, Gran?' Willard asked.

'Because Sid doesn't need me now, after all,' she smiled sadly. 'Not now he's got *real* circus stars.'

'Er ... um ... I hope you don't mind?' he apologized, hesitantly.

'Not at all,' she fibbed, trying to hide her disappointment but not succeeding.

She had looked forward to performing all the circus acts she had learned in the last few days. And she was never likely to get the chance to perform in a circus again. She sighed but put a brave face on it.

And her friends were disappointed too. For they also had looked forward to being circus performers, if only on this one occasion. But now, as they weren't needed, they could only watch the contest as part of the audience.

Sid went back to the dressing-room for a cup of coffee and, soon afterwards, disaster struck! Or rather, Peck A. Daily struck – via the Scunner! But if it was bad luck for all the competitors, including Sid and his troupe, it turned out to be good luck for Super Gran and her troupe!

'Okay, Tub?' whispered the Scunner, dressed as a clown.

They were emerging from the two dressing-rooms into which they had sneaked minutes earlier, in disguise, to nobble the performers' teas and coffees.

'Y-y-yes,' murmured the blushing, highly embarrassed Tub. 'B-but I still think you sh-should've got s-someone else to go into *that* dressing-room!'

'Aw, but you look so convincing,' the Scunner insisted as he tweaked Tub's cheek playfully. 'And so sweet, too!'

'Gerroff!' he muttered, blushing worse than ever.

He was disguised as a glamorous circus showgirl, complete with a little blue ballet skirt, black tights, a blonde wig and tons of make-up. And he *had* been convincing, for the women in the dressing-room hadn't noticed him!

But he couldn't rush out of the Big Top quickly enough to reach a spare tent and change back into his own clothes again.

'Huh!' he muttered. 'The things I get involved in!'

But while Tub was hurriedly changing the Scunner was unhurriedly loitering outside the dressing-rooms in the Big Top, awaiting the results of their tea-nobbling. Would it be successful?

As he waited his thoughts returned to his meeting with Daily, the previous day at his villa after his 'demob' from the RAF, when they had discussed the job . . .

'Look, Scunner, I want to win these Championships. It means a lot to me. Financially. Whoever wins gets big audiences afterwards. So there's lots of lovely lolly in it for me. And for you, too.'

'Is that a fact?' said the Scunner, wondering if perhaps he should go into the circus business, himself.

'But apart from the money,' Daily went on, 'I just like winning contests. But the only way to guarantee winning contests – is to cheat! And that's where you come in. Right? Right!'

'I don't see why I should come in anywhere,' the Scunner had retorted bravely. 'I don't need to do your dirty work for you.'

'Please yourself,' Daily said, sweetly, then added: 'But I should warn you it's not unknown for me to set my circus lions on to anyone who doesn't do little favours for me. And I'm not "lion" about that either, ha, ha, ha!' He chortled nastily and a shiver ran up and down the Scunner's spine. 'Right? Right!'

'You don't scare me!' The Scunner was defiant. ''Cos I know for a fact there aren't any animal acts in this year's competition. So you won't have any lions with you. See?'

'That's what you think! I won't be bringing them with me for an act but I'll be bringing four of 'em along – just to make sure you do as you're told. Right? Right!'

'Okay, what d'you want me to do?' the Scunner rasped, suddenly defeated and suddenly eager to keep in Daily's good books. 'And what's in it for me. I mean – financially?'

'Ah, I thought you'd see it my way, Campbell,' Daily said, all friendly again. 'Don't worry, you'll be paid all right. Well paid. Afterwards.'

'So what do I do?' he asked.

'It couldn't be easier,' smiled Daily. 'You just slip into the dressing-rooms and slip a little something into everyone's tea during the tea-break, before the contest starts.'

'Nobble them? Is that all?' The Scunner smiled. 'There's nothing to it. I won't even need the Muscles for that, just Tub.'

'Yeah, but it's important to do it before I arrive with my performers. Otherwise some suspicious people might suspect little old me of doing it. And we don't want that, do we?'

'Don't worry. Leave it to me,' he said confidently . . .

And now, a day later, the Scunner saw the results of his tea-nobbling. For as he stood there his performers, one by one, came staggering out of the dressing-rooms clutching their stomachs, in search of the nearest toilets. They all felt extremely sick and their greenish faces clearly showed it!

'Ooh! Oooo-oh! Save me, save me!' they cried.

And it was just about then the clown-faced Daily and his performers arrived.

'Oh, dearie me,' he said, 'everyone's sick? How sad!'

He and the rest of his troupe – including Wendy – were dressed and wearing their make-up all ready to take part in the contest, confident that there would be no contest.

'Sorry we're late. We were held up in the traffic,' he lied.

He had made sure he kept well out of the way while the Scunner and Tub were doing their nobbling. And although the competition organizers eyed him with suspicion and were sure he was behind it they had no proof and they knew that he was nowhere near the dressing-rooms at the time.

'Oh, dearie me, if everyone's ill,' he said to the chief official, with a confident smirk, 'that means the contest will have to be cancelled. Right? Right!'

'Yes . . . er . . . ah . . . I suppose so,' the chief official replied as he and his fellow-organizers exchanged glances. What else could they do? The contestants were too ill to take part.

'In that case,' Daily said, 'that means I've won. By default. Or by a walkover or whatever you call it.'

'What?' The officials were taken aback at this. 'But . . . but . . . they stuttered, not quite knowing what to say or do.

'It stands to reason,' he explained, with a smirk. 'My circus is the only one fit to take part so it must be the winner!'

He had won the argument and the contest!

'Now wasn't it lucky for us we were held up in the traffic?' he gloated

'Yes, wasn't it!' the chief official growled.

Sid Scouse came staggering out of the toilet just then, still looking green about the gills and still clutching his sore stomach. He was too ill to take part in the discussion but he was able to take the news to Super Gran who, with the rest of the audience, had been waiting patiently for the contest to start.

'Looks . . . as if . . . Daily's . . . won,' he said.

And he explained about the performers being ill and how Daily had claimed victory in the competition.

'What? That's what *he* thinks!' Super Gran cried as she leapt over the barrier into the ring, calling on her friends to join her. 'Come on, folks!'

And while her astonished friends left their seats and crossed the ring in a less excitable way, she went racing across it to reach the officials before it was too late.

'Wait! Stop! Don't award Daily the contest!' she yelled.

'Huh? Why not?' the officials said.

'Yes, madam, why not?' Daily repeated, indignantly.

''Cos my friends out there in the ring, and I, are registered to take part in the contest, for Scouse's Circus.'

'What?' an official burst out laughing, 'You? A little old lady? And a postman and a lot of other old ladies?' he added as the others joined them.

But the officials were soon assured that this was indeed part of Sid's temporary circus staff.

'Right,' they declared, as the audience became more

and more restive and began demanding refunds on their money. 'Let's get on with the contest. Daily and Scouse both have a walkover into the final round. Let's go . . .'

'I object!' Daily screamed but the officials just ignored him.

'Yippee!' cried Mrs Preston as she and the rest of the troupe happily trooped into the dressing-rooms to get ready. 'We're performing in the circus after all.'

'Aye, that's great,' Super Gran agreed. Then she frowned, thoughtfully. 'But I think I saw the Scunner lurking about out here. I wonder if he had something to do with everyone being sick? I'll bet he had.'

16 It's No Contest!

Super Gran and her friends emerged from the dressing-rooms and entered the ring with Sid where they were joined by Daily's performers, to be introduced to the audience.

The ringmaster, dressed in a red coat, black trousers and a top hat was in charge of announcements and introduced the leaders of the two teams in the final. Then Sid and Daily faced each other in the centre of the sawdust ring and shook hands while their teams stood around behind them; Daily's performers being full of confidence, but Sid's, apart from Super Gran, looking shy and overawed by the occasion.

Jings! There's Wendy, Super Gran thought, recognizing her despite her glamorous circus gear – false eyelashes, spangled costume and fish-net tights. And she really looked like a circus performer now.

I just hope she's happier with Daily than she was with Sid, Super Gran thought. Oh well, good luck to her. And good luck to us, too!

'May the best team win,' said Sid, shaking Daily's hand.

'Well that's us!' Daily chortled nastily. 'You've *no* chance. Not with that grotty lot!'

Sid secretly agreed with him and knew that his only

hope was Super Gran, although he could hardly expect her to perform like an expert in every act. He sighed. This certainly looked like the final performance of Scouse's Circus.

Daily's mob were now waving confidently to the noisy, applauding, cheering audience and Super Gran looked over at their leader and wondered again about him.

He was wearing his clown's make-up, of course, but she couldn't help thinking there was something just a tiny bit familiar about him. *Had* she seen him somewhere before? She was sure she had. Not just on the day of registration but before that. Some time before, and somewhere unconnected with the circus.

She shrugged and put it out of her mind. There were more important things to think about.

Then Sid's circus left the ring again leaving one of Daily's acts there, to have first go. And as Sid walked out, with Super Gran, he smiled a wan, but encouraging smile at her.

'Good luck,' he said. 'Against Daily's circus – you and your friends'll need it!'

Then he left her and approached Walt and Pepe who had by now also recovered slightly from their sore stomachs.

'What chance have we got, lads? Not much, eh? I *don't* mind Super Gran. But the rest of that motley crew! Whew!'

'Yeah,' Walt and Pepe sympathized.

Super Gran's friends left the Big Top to collect the

various pieces of equipment – stilts, balancing balls, unicycles and trampolines – which they needed for their acts, from Sid's trailer outside.

And so – at last! – the Circus Championships got under way.

Six members of the Daily circus began by performing a balancing act, climbing on top of each other to form a pyramid, while the audience clapped and cheered.

'Eight out of ten,' the judges at the side of the ring announced, and this was marked up on Daily's scoreboard as Super Gran led her friends into the ring to do their first act.

The Scunner and Tub – now dressed in his own clothes, but still blushing furiously! – reported backstage to Daily and the Scunner held his hand out.

'Right, pay up! We've nobbled the opposition.'

'But Super Gran's in the opposition now,' Daily pointed out. 'You'll need to nobble *her*, somehow.'

'What?' he yelled. 'You didn't tell me *she* was taking part.'

'It's a long story. I'll tell you afterwards. In the meantime she *is* taking part – so get rid of her.'

'But, how? How?' he asked.

'Don't stand there imitating a Red Indian, just think of something. Quickly! And just nobble *her*, never mind her geriatric friends. Right? Right!'

'Oh . . . all right,' he growled, reluctantly. 'I'll think of something.'

He was annoyed at not getting paid. After all it wasn't his fault if Super Gran was now taking part, was it?

Daily left him and Tub and went back to join the rest of his troupe to await his own turn in the ring.

'What'll we do, Uncle?' Tub asked, but the Scunner shrugged.

'We can hardly run round the ring with a cup of nobbled tea, trying to persuade the old bat to drink it, can we? We'll just have to wait and see what happens.'

'That's them started now,' Tub said, pointing to the ring.

Mrs Preston and a group of pensioners were supposed to be performing on the trampoline. But instead of bouncing up and down on it one of them, being too heavy, had jumped right through it, which put an end not only to the act but also to the trampoline!

'Ha, ha, ha!' said the audience. And:

'One point out of ten!' said the judges. But then, after deciding it was possibly supposed to be a comedy act, they awarded an extra point!

The Dailys entered the ring again, led by Wendy. This was a novelty item called 'Oodles of Poodles', a dog-training act, although the dogs were merely Dailys wearing poodle ears and noses who crouched, panting, on the sawdust floor and pretended to jump through hoops held at ground level.

The act was greeted by laughter and applause from the appreciative audience.

'Eight out of ten,' announced the judges, while Daily sneered at Sid, standing nearby.

'At least our act is *supposed* to be funny, unlike yours.'

Sid groaned and wished the whole thing was finished so he could creep quietly away from Daily, the audience, the circus and everyone connected with it. It was a complete shambles.

The two scoreboards were rapidly changing as each side gained points. But for every eight or nine points out of ten which Daily's performers got, Sid's got only two or three! And they only got those because the judges felt sorry for them!

And so, after four acts, Daily's circus had thirty-four points while Sid's only had nine! He looked at the scoreboard, and shuddered.

Next, one of the Dailys did his strong-man act and tore a phone directory in half. But Postman Pugh, to outdo him and gain a few extra points, tried to do the same while riding a unicycle! But didn't succeed!

By mistake he had grabbed one of the trick cycles which he found outside the ring. And it would have been difficult enough doing it as he had intended, but trying to do it on a trick bike whose one wheel wobbled to the side and whose saddle threw him up in the air was just too much. He fell off and the directory thumped him on the head.

'Ouch! Ooyah!' he yelled. And:

'Ha, ha, ha,' went the audience.

'Nine points to Daily,' declared the judges, 'and two to Scouse – for their usual comedy act!'

Which put Daily even further ahead of Sid.

'Are *all* Scouse's acts comedy acts?' the ringmaster asked, through his microphone, and the audience howled with laughter.

The embarrassed Sid went in search of Super Gran who seemed to have disappeared recently.

'We've had it,' he said. 'It doesn't look as if we're even good enough to come second! Can't you do something to help?'

'Aye, but I've been watching that wee bachle the Scunner. He and Daily have been cooking up something else, I'm sure of it. Maybe I should read their minds and find out . . .'

'Not now,' Sid interrupted. 'All our acts are terrible, I just knew they would be. Can't *you* start performing – please!'

'Jings!' She looked up at the scoreboard. 'We're not doing too well, are we? It's time I got in there and earned some points, isn't it?'

'Yeah, we need them,' he agreed mournfully.

But he didn't hold out much hope. The Dailys were too far ahead now for them to catch up, even with Super Gran performing.

'Just watch this, laddie,' she said determinedly.

Gladys had entered the ring and was trying to be a tumbler. But she only managed a very half-hearted cartwheel before falling flat on her face. The audience howled with laughter once again but this time Super Gran called out:

'That was our comedy version, folks – now watch the proper version!'

Then she zoomed back and forward across the ring performing handsprings, cartwheels and somersaults – all at Super-speed! The audience gasped in amazement.

She ended her act by leaping on to a mini trampoline in the centre of the ring and bouncing high in

the air, doing double and triple somersaults on the way!

'Nine points,' the judges announced, 'plus one for the comedy part of the performance!'

The Dailys now did a cowboy act with whips, spinning lassoes and knives thrown at Wendy, who was on a revolving target, by a blindfolded knife-thrower.

'If only Walt's act was like that,' Sid sighed, as Wendy and the cowboys earned another nine points.

Then Mrs Preston – wearing a crash helmet! – entered the ring to do a juggling act with three coloured billiard balls, and Super Gran joined her. And after she dropped the balls on her helmet – gaining a point for comedy, as usual! – Super Gran took over. But instead of juggling three balls she juggled with twenty-three, keeping all of them in the air at once. And this gained them another nine points, to add to Mrs Preston's one point.

17   Flyin'...

And this was the way the competition proceeded. Each time Gladys, Mrs Preston, Pugh and the others entered the ring Super Gran went with them. And after they had fooled around and made a right old mess of the act she would take over and do it properly, giving the judges and the audience two different versions of each act, the 'comedy' version and the real version.

In addition she did a few acts on her own, like low-wire walking and stilt-walking, which she'd done at Sid's circus. So, between one thing and another, she was the cause of their team's points catching up, to some extent, with Daily's.

But what also helped to close the gap between the teams was the fact that Daily's performers, amazed at the sight of Super Gran's stunts, lost some of their confidence. Which meant that they gained only five or six points for each act now, instead of the eight or nine they had previously gained.

The exception to this was when Daily entered the ring to perform his clown act. This consisted of him and one of his city-suited associates pretending to throw fire buckets full of water over each other.

'Look out – it's bath night . . .' they yelled as they

threw the buckets containing coloured confetti instead of water.

And to end the act, and in an effort to dodge the thrown bucket itself, Daily ducked aside and rushed out of the ring towards one of the king poles. Then he ran two or three metres straight up it before throwing himself off in a backward flip over the other man's head, to land on his feet again on the ground.

And this gained him another eight points out of ten.

But then it was time for each side to do their 'star' turn, a 'big' act which would earn them no less than fifty points.

'But what're we going to do?' Sid asked Super Gran, 'I never thought about it before. I never thought we'd reach the final!'

Super Gran looked up at the roof of the Big Top. 'Well, Sid, I've always fancied trying the trapeze, as I told you, before.'

'What? You're joking!' he gasped.

She pointed up at the two trapeze swings, their adjacent platforms and the narrow rope ladders which led towards them.

'Joking? Just you watch me!' she said. 'But it's quite a climb up the ladder, isn't it?'

'It's thirty metres up!' he told her. 'It's a slow climb but a quick descent, you just slide down the rope at the side.'

'I'll remember that,' she said as she left him and ran across the ring to the ladder.

'Hey, wait . . .' he began, but she ignored him and ran off.

And when Willard saw where his Gran was headed he led the other children in the audience in cheering her on. Although Edison wasn't so sure it was a good idea. Not at her age.

But Daily, who had been loitering near by, overheard Sid's comment about the rope and he moved round the outside of the ring, a thoughtful look creasing his white clown's face. Then he spotted the Scunner approaching, from backstage.

As the spotlight shone on Super Gran and she started to climb the ladder, Willard suddenly shouted:

'Hey, Gran! You've never been on a trapeze before!'

'Neither I have!' she yelled back. 'Exciting, isn't it?'

A long, loud roll on the orchestra's drum accompanied her as she climbed, while below her Edison put her hands over her eyes, unable to watch.

'I hope she'll be all right. I didn't know she hadn't done it before or I'd've stopped her.'

'What – you?' Willard snorted. 'Nobody can stop Gran once she makes up her mind to do something.'

While, at the side of the ring:

'You haven't nobbled her, Campbell!' Daily stormed.

'Er . . . ah . . . um . . . no, not yet.'

'I told you to put her out of action and now she's heading for the trapeze. She'll do something spectacular up there and that'll get lousy Scousy some valuable points. And there's fifty on offer for her performance. That's their "star" turn!'

148

'What's the problem?' the Scunner asked. 'Just get one of your mob to have a go on it after her and he'll win the fifty points too. Easy!'

'But I don't have a trapeze artist, idiot! So Scouse'll get ahead of me.'

His expression changed to one of determination.

'But he'd better not, if *you* know what's good for you. For a start, you won't get paid. And for a finish – it'll be a finish for you. And I'm not "lion" about it. Gettit?'

The evil smirk on Daily's face convinced the Scunner that he really would set his lions on him. He shuddered.

'But . . . but what d'you want me to do?'

'Cut her trapeze rope,' Daily said, evilly.

'What?' The Scunner couldn't believe his ears. He pointed upwards. 'You mean, up there . . .?'

'No, not the actual trapeze rope,' Daily explained. 'You couldn't get up there, and even if you did everyone would see you doing it. No, I mean the little retaining one that holds the rope she'll slide down, at the end of her performance.'

'But she'll fall like a stone!' he gasped with horror, his face going as white as Daily's clown face. Even *he* drew the line at that. 'But it . . . it . . .' he stammered, 'it would be goodbye to the old bat. No, I can't do it. I *won't* do it. You're not on!'

By now Super Gran had reached the platform and was waving again to the audience below.

'You all look so wee, down there!' she yelled.

She pulled the swing towards her and sat on it. Then

149

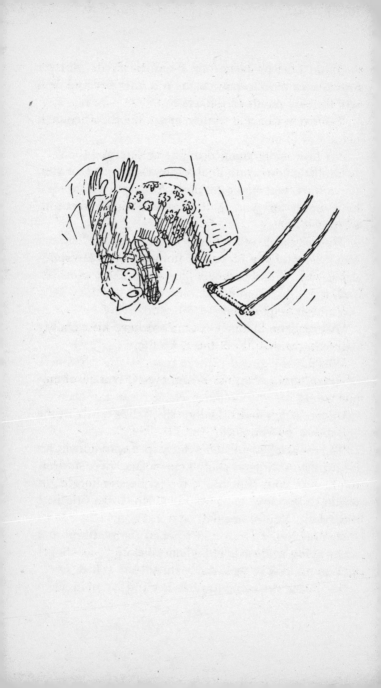

she pushed herself away from the platform and started swinging back and forth on the trapeze, going farther and farther out from the platform with each swing and going higher and higher into the roof of the Big Top.

Having got the knack of swinging outward she surprised her audience by leaping off it on to the other swing but catching hold of it easily, much to the audience's relief. And again she waved down to them.

'Whew!' they gasped, and:

'Wow!' gasped Willard and Edison.

But: 'I'm relying on you, Campbell. Cut her rope!'

'No way!' The Scunner's face was still as white as Daily's.

'I'm ordering you!'

'Ordering me? Who d'you think you are, Daily, Flight Sergeant Brain of the RAF?'

'Who?'

'Never mind. I'm just not doing it, money or no money.'

'Lions . . .' reminded Daily.

'Lions or no lions,' snapped the Scunner.

But Daily's evil smile was replaced by a sly look.

'Oh, you were worrying about her falling? But she won't, she'll only fall into her safety net. I forgot to mention that. See . . .' he pointed upwards, 'it's between her and the ground and it'll break her fall. Honestly.'

The safety net was held by four poles and was about eight metres above the ring.

'I don't care. I'm not doing it. She *still* might get hurt and I'd be lost without the old bat.'

The 'old bat' continued to do some more swings back and forth and then did a mid-air spin while flying between the two trapezes.

The Scunner never imagined he'd ever hear himself saying that about her. He must, he thought, be getting soft in his old age!

'And besides, she helped to get me out of the air force.'

He pushed the waiting acts aside as he rushed away from Daily and out of the Big Top's rear entrance.

Daily, taken aback at this, had a look of utter amazement on his face. The Scunner had actually refused to do his dirty work for him and even the threat of being fed to the lions hadn't made him change his mind.

But then he spotted Wendy who came teetering on her high heels out of the women's dressing-room, ready for her next act.

'Ah! Wonderful Wendy! The very person,' he said, putting his arm around her bare shoulders. 'You're so grateful I allowed you to join my circus, aren't you?'

She nodded, smiling. 'You know I am, Mr Daily.'

'And you'd like to do me a little favour to pay me back for my kindness, wouldn't you?'

She nodded again, still smiling. 'I would, Mr Daily.'

'Well, now's your big chance. I want you to cut Super Gran's retaining rope . . .'

'What?' The smile froze on her face. She was shocked. She was horrified.

'Shhhhh!' he hushed her. 'It's a secret. We want to surprise the audience . . .'

'You'll surprise more than the audience!' she snapped. 'You'll surprise Super Gran, as well!'

'Ah, but she knows we're doing it,' he lied. 'And she'll only fall into her safety net. She won't be hurt. You know that.'

'But what's the idea?' she asked, suspiciously.

'It's to give the audience a little thrill,' he explained. 'You know how they like to have something unexpected happen in a circus? They like to think a performer's in danger and is falling to her death, when she's not really.'

He wore an innocent expression on his clown's face which fooled her completely. Audiences *did* like to be thrilled, she knew, and if the safety net was safely under Super Gran then she wouldn't really be hurt by falling into it. And especially if she knew she was going to fall.

'Oh, all right,' she agreed, 'I'll do it.'

'You know what to do,' he said, giving her a penknife out of his pocket. She nodded and made her way to the retaining rope.

But as soon as she left him he contacted one of his tentmen and whispered:

'Charlie, drop the safety net. Take one of your lads and kick two of its poles over. When I give you the nod. Right? Right!'

'Right, boss,' Charlie said as he moved off.

Daily rubbed his hands together with undisguised glee.

'That interfering old pest will really fall now. The net won't help her. Revenge is sweet!'

He approached another of his men.

'Jack, fetch the boys and get the cage into the ring.'

'But I didn't think we were doing the lion-taming act, boss.'

'Don't think! Just do as you're told. Right? Right!'

'Right, boss.' Jack shrugged. 'You're the boss, boss.'

18 . . . to the Lion!

The man left the Big Top with three mates and returned, minutes later, with the sides of a open-topped animal cage. They then proceeded to piece it together and position it below Super Gran's safety net and at the side of the ring, near the trapeze ladder.

Next they attached an open-meshed tunnel which led from the cage and out of the ring to an open flap at the rear of the Big Top. And finally they carried a chair and a whip into the cage then added four tall metal stools, which they placed all around it.

And while all this was going on Super Gran continued her act aloft as she flew through the air between the two trapeze swings performing somersaults, double somersaults and triple somersaults, during which she reached speeds of up to sixty miles an hour!

'Whooo!' the audience gasped.

And as this was Scouse's 'star turn' she was determined to do her very best, not only to gain the maximum points, if possible, but also to give her audience – and the judges – a memorable performance. So she now thrilled them, thirty metres below her, by doing a headstand on the narrow trapeze bar.

'Wow!' gasped Willard, Edison and the crowd.

She now swung gently back and forward on the

swing, upside down, hanging on by her right foot only. Then she switched to her left foot only.

'Ooooh!' the audience gasped and held its communal breath.

They had seen trapeze acts before but none like this one, performed by a little old lady!

Then, to complete the act, she launched herself into the space between the two swings with a backward somersault and reached the platform where she bowed and waved to the clapping, cheering, whistling audience.

She took hold of the rope beside the ladder to slide down it. But, below her, Wendy crouched with the penknife in her hand and looked towards Daily, awaiting his nod.

He nodded not only to Wendy, but also to his accomplices Charlie and Jack who, like her, had been awaiting his signal.

'A little extra surprise, Wendy dear,' he murmured quietly. 'You didn't know about this one! And neither did Super Gran!'

He looked up at the trapeze platform as he said this and laughed quietly, but evilly.

Then four things happened almost simultaneously. Super Gran started sliding down the rope; Wendy cut the rope which held it; Charlie and his mate kicked away two of the poles supporting the safety net; and Jack opened a gate at the rear of the Big Top.

This released four lions from their cage outside and allowed them to run through the tunnel and into the cage in the ring. The audience gasped and screamed as the lions appeared, and as Super Gran fell.

'Jings! Help!' she yelled, but had the presence of mind to throw herself inwards, towards the safety net.

And as she continued falling towards it, twenty-odd metres below her, at speed, she had the sense to know how to fall properly. She twisted herself round and curled her body into a ball so that she would land safely in the net, with her shoulders taking the blow and with her legs in the air. But:

'Oh no! Help!' she cried as she hit the loosened, collapsing net but kept falling towards the ground, taking it with her.

She landed, winded, in the cage amongst the four snarling, prowling lions. But at least her fall was broken when she landed on the back of one of them – although that didn't do a lot for the lion's temper!

The audience gasped, screamed and jumped to their feet in horror as Super Gran slipped off the lion's back and landed on *her* back, in the cage.

'Oh no!' screamed Edison.

'Gran!' yelled Willard.

'We'll have to rescue her, somehow!' gasped Inventor Black.

'Your new gadget,' Edison yelled, pulling his arm to remind him about it, 'your slow-motion machine. You've got it with you!'

'Yes, somewhere . . .' He fiddled in his pockets, searching for it. 'Let's see, now, it was in my jacket pocket when we left home. Or was it my trouser pocket . . .?'

157

'Hurry up,' Edison urged, seeing that Super Gran was groggy as she lay on the floor of the cage at the lions' feet.

Her eyes were misty at first from the fall but her Super-sight was helping them to clear. But as they did so she could see she was trapped in the cage with the lions prowling around her, with the one on whose back she had landed looking particularly annoyed!

And Black still searched for his gadget!

'It's about the size of a small torch or a pocket camera or a mini transis . . .'

'You told us that before,' Willard interrupted. 'Just hurry up and find it!'

Black, at last, pulled a small gadget from one of his pockets. 'Ah, here it is . . .'

He switched it on – and the tiniest flicker of light emerged from it and a barely audible, tinny voice said: 'My batteries . . . My batt . . . My . . .'

'Oh-oh, this *is* the torch, that's no good.' He tried again. 'Ah, here it is.'

He pulled a second gadget from his pocket, pointed it towards the lions in the cage and pressed a button. But there was a loud click and a tiny tinny voice said: 'Smile please! Say cheese!'

'Oh no, that's my new super-duper camera. That's no use either. Except we've now got a picture of Super Gran in the cage with the lions . . .'

'Hurry up!' Willard yelled, in exasperation.

He pulled a third gadget from his pocket, pointed it at the cage and switched it on. But a strident, tinny voice said: 'Listen to Chis-le-ton Radio – for DJ Pete Saik.'

'For Pete's sake!' screamed Edison, as she joined Black in searching through his pockets for the elusive invention.

She could see the snarling lions prowling ever nearer to Super Gran who was now propped up on one elbow but was still dizzy from her fall.

'Got it!' he exclaimed, at last, as he pulled forth the fourth gadget from his numerous pockets and pointed it at the lions.

'Don't worry, Super Gran,' he yelled, 'this'll slow 'em down.'

'Yeah, *if* it works!' snorted Willard.

Two of the lions were now leaping up and down from their high stools, a third one was snarling at her and the fourth one was pawing the air in front of her, menacingly. This last one, having recovered from acting as her unofficial mattress, was showing her how much it had resented the role – and how sharp its teeth were!

Suddenly all their movements, their pawing, snarling, leaping and teeth-showing, went into slow motion as Black's machine worked.

'Whew!' he breathed as he mopped the sweat from his brow, and smiled. 'There – it worked!'

He hadn't been too sure of its success but now he looked extremely pleased with himself.

But, seconds later, he looked horrified again as he realized that the machine's beam had also hit Super

Gran. Which meant that although she jumped to her feet, to escape from the cage, she could only move as slowly as the lions were moving and was therefore unable to outrun them. So having the lions in slow motion hadn't helped her at all!

'I told you it wouldn't work,' Willard said with a smug 'I told you so' look on his face.

'It did work,' Black insisted, 'it's just that I aimed it at the whole cage instead of aiming it just at the lions.'

'Then reverse it,' Edison said, 'and start all over again, but without hitting Super Gran this time. And hurry up about it!'

'Good idea,' he agreed and did as she said.

Within seconds the lions were brought back to normal, then slowed down again. While Super Gran was brought back to normal but was allowed to stay normal.

Then, picking up the chair to defend herself – the way she'd seen real lion-tamers do – and the whip to crack it at them, she soon had the four lions jumping docilely – but slowly! – back on to their stools.

'You wouldn't hurt wee Super Gran, now would you?'

She patted each of the slowly-snarling lions on the head, in turn, at which one of them made a sound like a giant 'miaow'.

'Aw!' she said, as she put her arm around its neck and cuddled it.

Then the others saw this, became jealous and 'miaowed' too, so that she'd have to cuddle them, also!

The audience seemed to have been holding its breath for ages while she'd been in the cage at the mercy of the lions. But now they could breathe easily again. And they could also burst into wild applause and loud cheers, which they did.

She acknowledged their cheers and then she spoke quietly to each of the lions, in turn, before she left the cage.

'You didn't really want to harm wee Super Gran, did you? No, of course you didn't.'

The ringmaster now set some of the circus hands to work.

First of all they re-erected the two fallen safety net poles to put the net back in place again. And secondly they enticed the slowly-moving lions out of the cage in the ring and along the tunnel to their cage outside the Big Top.

'The slow-motion effects,' Black explained to Willard and Edison, 'will wear off in a little while.'

Then the judges announced:

'Super Gran's points for performing on the trapeze are – fifty out of fifty!'

Then, after the audience had cheered this news, they added:

'And we've decided that, as a bonus for doing her lion-taming act – even if it was rather forced upon her! – she should get an extra twenty points.'

The audience went mad as these seventy points were marked up on Scouse's scoreboard which now actually put them ahead of Daily – by forty-nine points!

'I object!' he said, loudly, until one of the officials asked:

'But who put the lions into the ring, in the first place?'

'Curses!' he muttered.

His plans had been thwarted. Not only had he *not* got his revenge on Super Gran but she had also won the fifty points for her star turn on the trapeze.

'But I'll win, yet . . .!' he said, confidently.

19   'Runny' Egg!

Daily still had his star turn to come. And once he did it and earned *his* fifty points his circus once again would come out on top and would just manage to win the Championships.

'It's my "star turn" now,' he called out to the ringmaster and the judges. 'I'll do my party piece – my vertical pole-running. But this time I'll run up the king pole – to the very top!'

'Oh-oh,' a crestfallen Sid said to Super Gran. 'He'll get fifty points for that, no bother. It's a speciality act that no one else can do.'

'Bet you *I* could do it,' she boasted with her usual lack of modesty.

'But you won't get the chance,' he told her, mournfully. 'You've had your chance at your star turn. So we've had it. Daily'll win after all.'

'Yes, Daily'll win, all right,' said the grinning Daily, overhearing them. 'Just watch this . . .'

And without another word he ran at one of the king poles, intending to run up it in his usual style. But this time his feet slipped off the pole when he was approximately four metres off the ground.

'He-elp . . .!' he yelled as he fell headlong.

But Super Gran zoomed towards the pole to catch

him before he hit the ground. 'Gotcha!' she yelled.

'Whew! Er . . . ah . . . um . . .,' he said, with no signs of gratitude.

He walked away from her into the ring again, to pace out his run, to have another go. Daily did not give in easily.

'Oh no,' Sid moaned, 'he'll do it this time, for sure.'

But when he went to run at the king pole this time he only managed a couple of paces before his ankle gave way and, with a yelp of pain, he fell to the ground.

'He must've twisted it, running up the pole,' Super Gran said.

He struggled to his feet and tried once more but his ankle was so bad he could only hobble on it, never mind run up vertical poles on it! So he had no option but to admit defeat.

'That's it!' Sid yelled, excitedly, 'we've won. We've won the Championships!'

He couldn't believe it. It was a miracle! And, despite what Wendy had said, miracles *did* still happen!

The ringmaster now persuaded Scouse's Circus – both the professional and amateur members of it – to enter the ring and take a bow, as the new circus champions. With Super Gran as the centre of attraction, of course.

But suddenly a tearful, mascara-run Wendy ran in to the ring to join them.

'Oh Sid – Super Gran,' she cried, 'can you ever forgive me for cutting that rope? I promise you I didn't know what was going to happen. He said you'd fall into the safety net and you knew all about it. But he didn't tell me he was going to drop the net. He lied to me, honestly.'

She looked so upset and angry with herself and she so badly wanted them to believe her that she looked rather pathetic. But Super Gran, with a quick flash of her mind-reading powers that confirmed she was telling the truth, smiled at her.

'Och, there's nothing to forgive, lassie. It was that wee bachle Daily's doing. I realize that.' She looked thoughtful. 'But I still think I know his face from somewhere. I just wish I could remember where.'

Sid put his arm round Wendy's shoulder and the two of them smiled at each other.

'Won't you come back to *my* circus, Wendy?'

'Of course I will, Sid, if you'll have me.'

'Of course I'll have you.'

'And if you've still *got* a circus!' She frowned.

'Of course I have,' he assured her. 'And after winning the Championships it won't be long till I've got all my stars – *and* my audiences! – back again. And it's all thanks to Super Gran.'

So Sid and Wendy were at least two people who were having a happy ending.

As the audience made their way out of the Big Top, Willard, Edison and Black left their seats to join the others in the ring.

'I'm sure I've seen Daily somewhere before,' said Super Gran. 'It was when he ran up those poles that reminded me.'

'Maybe he's in disguise, Gran,' Willard suggested.

'Yes,' Edison added, 'maybe he's someone you know, under the clown's face and the red nose.'

'Aye, you know,' she said, thoughtfully, 'I've only met him twice – here, today, and when we were registering – and he's been in his clown's outfit each time. So I've never seen him without it and I don't know what he really looks like.'

She turned to look for him and saw he was hobbling towards the exit, looking back over his shoulder, guiltily. He was obviously trying to slip away, to catch up with the rest of his mob who had already left.

'Hey, Daily!' she shouted. 'Come back here, will you. I've got something you'll be interested in.'

His curiosity overcame his desire to slink away. He turned and hobbled back towards her. 'What is it?'

She bent down and lifted up one of the fire buckets at the side of the ring.

'This!' she yelled, and made as if to throw its contents all over him, yelling: 'Look out, it's bath night . . .!'

And Daily, thinking it was part of his usual act, merely smiled and stood his ground. But it wasn't. It was real water this time and it not only soaked him to the skin but it also took his breath away, having been thrown with the whole of Super Gran's Super-strength.

'Ugh!' He gulped, trying to catch his breath.

This not only stopped him dead in his tracks, but also washed off his clown's thick make-up, revealing his normal face underneath. Then, before he could move, she leapt at him and pulled off his scarlet wig and his clown's red nose, snapping its elastic as she did so.

'Jings!' she yelled, with astonishment, recognizing him. 'It's Runny – Runny Egg. The cat burglar! Of course! It all comes back to me now!'

'A cat burglar?' yelled Willard.

'But who *is* he? Who's Runny Egg?' Edison asked.

'He's a thief I caught, some time ago, running straight up the wall of a Stately Home, to rob it. And that's why he's called Runny, 'cos he can run up walls! And he was imprisoned but he must have escaped.'

'Yeah,' muttered Daily/Runny when he finally recovered his breath. 'I did. And I've been waiting to get my own back on you. Nobody puts *me* away and gets away with it.'

'That's why I didn't recognize you. You weren't wearing your clown's face when you robbed that house.'

'And a circus is the perfect place to hide, isn't it?' said Edison. 'And especially in clown's make-up – it's the perfect disguise.'

Super Gran frowned. 'And my rope was cut, for revenge?'

Suddenly Daily, alias Runny, threw himself against one of the safety net poles nearby and knocked it down, causing the net to fall and entangling the unsuspecting Super Gran and the others beneath it.

'Jings! I'm all fankled up!' she yelled, as she struggled to free herself, to pursue Daily/Runny who was rushing from the Big Top, as fast as his hobbling gait would allow.

'You won't get me,' he yelled back at her as he escaped. 'You caught me the last time but you won't catch me this time.'

And all he'd have to do was grab the nearest parked car outside and make his getaway while she was still struggling under the net.

'Come back, you wee midden,' she yelled when she eventually managed to disentangle herself from the net, after a struggle, and ran after him. 'Stop! Thief! Police!'

But two people outside, in the circus area, heard the shout and thought she was after them!

The Scunner and Tub had slipped out of the Big Top earlier, to avoid Daily, and had been hanging around the other tents. But they didn't see him emerge and jump into his getaway car, they only heard Super Gran's yell and automatically thought she was shouting at them. So, without looking back, they took to their heels.

'Jings! That scunnery wee Scunner must have a right guilty conscience!' she said as she saw them go.

But all three crooks were out of luck and she stopped to laugh at them. For Daily's getaway car had turned out to be Sid's trick circus car, with the trailer still attached, and it wasn't getting him anywhere, fast!

'What the . . .?' he exclaimed, puzzled, as bits fell off the car and its steering wheel came off in his hands.

While the Scunner and Tub had also grabbed getaway vehicles but took two of the eccentric circus cycles by mistake!

'Huh . . .?' they exclaimed as their wheels wobbled and they rose and fell in their saddles with every pedal movement.

'Och, it'll be easy-peasy catching up with all three of those wee bachles,' Super Gran decided. 'At those speeds I'll catch them in two seconds flat!'

But then she had second thoughts about it.

'Och, no,' she laughed, 'I might as well give the wee bachles a chance, mightn't I?'

And so, sporting to the last, she too jumped on one of the trick bikes and chased after them in crazy, eccentric pursuit, knowing, as she pursued them – slowly and erratically! – across the common, that she could catch all of them just whenever she felt like it!

Some other Puffins

THE COMPUTER NUT

Betsy Byars

When Kate receives a message on her computer from a mysterious admirer, she hopes it's her secret crush, Willie Lomax. But she eventually discovers – no thanks to 'help' from her best friend Linda – that Willie is not the culprit. In fact, he turns out to be a resourceful computer sleuth when the two team up for hilarious close encounters with the alien comedian.

THE WITCH-CHILD

Imogen Chichester

Meet Mr and Mrs Gumblethrush, a wizard and witch, and their daughter Necromancy, who escapes to the world of ordinary children – a really funny fantasy story.

DOLPHIN ISLAND

Arthur C. Clarke

Johnny Clifton had never been happy living with Aunt Martha and her family for the twelve years since his parents had died when he was four. So when an intercontinental hovership breaks down outside the house, he stows away on it!